The Sweet Smell of
Mother's Milk-Wet Bodice

Cover artwork: Christine Lynn, "untitled" watercolour © 1998, CARCC. From
the collection of Joe Blades.
Copy edit by Elise Craft
Design and in-house editing by the publisher, Joe Blades.
Printed and bound in Canada by Sentinel Printing, Yarmouth, Nova Scotia

Simultaneously published as Broken Jaw Press eBook 31, ISBN 1-896647-73-1
(PDF, Acrobat Reader 3). Distribution via http://PublishingOnline.Com

BROKEN JAW PRESS
Box 596 Stn A   **www.brokenjaw.com**
Fredericton NB E3B 5A6   tel / fax 506 454-5127
Canada   jblades@nbnet.nb.ca

National Library of Canada Cataloguing in Publication Data
Uma Parameswaran
        The sweet smell of Mother's milk-wet bodice

ISBN 1-896647-72-3

        I. Title.

PS8581.A688S94 2001   C813'.54   C2001-901130-X
PR9199.3.U42S94 2001

The Sweet Smell of Mother's Milk-Wet Bodice

Uma Parameswaran

Fredericton • Canada

Acknowledgements

I would like to thank:

my husband and daughter for nagging me into spending more time on my creative writing;

Mamata Misra, founder of SAHELI: An Organization for Asian Families, Austin TX, for inviting me to read from the work-in-progress to the members of SAHELI, who gave me useful feedback;

Colonel Ram Jain, and my colleagues in India — Jasbir Jain and Malashri Lal — for helping me with details about Jaipur;

and most appreciatively, my publisher, Joe Blades, for readily accepting the typescript.

*This book is for my husband
and his dream of establishing a help centre
for South Asian Canadian women in Winnipeg.*

Foreword

I have lived and worked in Winnipeg for over thirty years. That is a long time, and as is natural for anyone with an activist spark, I have been on numerous committees and organizations that deal with ethnocultural, women's and writers' issues. I have heard numerous life-stories, each of which would make for a poignant novel. Though I have never had the time to concentrate on my writing, characters jostle around in my head, and one of them occasionally surfaces from the subconscious to the conscious despite my lack of devotion to my Muse.

Last year I had occasion to speak to Mamata Misra of SAHELI, a support group for South Asian women in Austin, Texas. She sent me a newspaper clipping from Bombay's *The Indian Express*. It spoke of women from India in the United States who were ill-treated or abandoned by their husbands. The correspondent quoted a South Asian American women's group as reporting that there have been "an increasing number of cases of women being served divorce papers within a year of coming to the U.S." Newspapers tend to be sensationalistic, we know, but in cases of violence against women and children, even one case is one too many in my thinking. The news item set three characters in my head clamouring to be heard — I have named them Ita Gill, Amita Eggill and Namita Neggill.

They are typical of women in all ethnocultural communities and in the overall social fabric. All three come as sponsored wives of landed immigrants, all three have unhappy abusive relationships, all three are kept in isolation from the ethnocultural community by their husbands, and all three get out of the abusive relationship. All three are single, and not because they want to be single. Individually, they represent three typical case histories. Collectively, they celebrate the will to survive, and our social safety nets.

This novella is a story of one of these characters. Namita surfaced from my subconscious onto my computer screen for several reasons. One, because the newspaper item had brought her racing to the surface of my consciousness and two, because her story is about an urgent need to recognize what has been accomplished and what needs to be addressed. This story is a tribute to the dedicated people who run women's shelters and women's organizations. It is a story of our cities, of the social assistance and other safety nets that picked her up and helped her back to her feet, and of the legal system that in the final count failed her. Between the lines, it speaks of the changes we need to make in our laws to build a better Canada.

The characters in this book are composites of lifestories heard and imagined over the years. As in my play, *Rootless but Green are the Boulevard Trees*, these are characters who go through experiences common to many immigrant families. To date, I have made all my major characters Indo-Canadian Hindus who live in Winnipeg, because that is a milieu I know well.

Though it is a complete novella, in my mind this book is an excerpt from a larger novel in which I wish to take Namita's story further and develop issues that are only glanced at in this work.

One line of development in the yet-to-be-completed novel is to show how lawyers and the law let her down in various ways. How can a new immigrant in an abusive relationship, without friend or family or knowledge of the new environment, be allowed to be divorced without spousal support? How can the legal process ignore such basic and well-documented patterns as the abused-woman syndrome of withdrawing charges of violence, and ethnocultural attitudes of dependency? It is time for changes to be made in the legal process. I would like to see laws that would place roadblocks to an immigrant being a party in a divorce-suit during the first two years of her or his stay in Canada. This would ensure that the parties have time to know their way around and be settled in the new country, before they have to cope with the trauma of divorce.

Moreover, anyone who sponsors a person into Canada takes an

oath to be financially responsible for that person for a minimum of five years. It is time the system makes these sponsors pay, the same as it should "deadbeat dads" who are delinquent in their child-support payments.

This novella came to be completed in its present form because of an external stimulus. I started writing the story as a novel last year after my trip to Austin, but shelved it because of my professional commitments at the university. Then, an e-mail came from out of the blue inviting me to be a speaker at a fundraising event for the Emily Stowe Shelter for Women in Toronto. It was as though Saraswati (Hindu Goddess and Muse) was at my elbow, chiding me about not using "that one talent which is death to hide" as Milton said. The story poured itself out over one marathon weekend at the computer early in January, and was revised several times over the next few weeks.

Uma Parameswaran
Winnipeg, Manitoba
March 2001

P.S.   I feel impelled to add a postscript at the galley-proof stage of this book's production. Last month, the Department of Family Services of the provincial government suddenly announced that it would stop funding the direct services offered by Immigrant Women's Association of Manitoba. This means that such services as counselling, English-language classes, and Parent-Child Outreach, will have to be closed down, or moved to non-immigrant agencies. Tomorrow's Namitas will have one more strike against them as they struggle to survive in a new environment.

May 2001

Chapter One

"Okay, girl, come along with me," Krista patted Namita on her back.

"Today we'll go for a long drive. Get up, and away we go." She gave Namita another hearty push.

As Namita got up from her chair in the lounge, Krista looked at her from head to toe. "That cardigan should be enough, it's a warm day. And high time too, seeing July is almost on us. Good you have your runners on, so off we go," she boomed in her cheerful voice. To the receptionist at the front desk, she said she'd step in for a moment to drop off the new girl she was taking with her, but otherwise she was through for the day.

They went to the rear of the building, and Krista opened the passenger door of her faded blue Acadian.

"Get in, and here, hold this till I come around," she pulled out the seat belt and handed the buckle to Namita to hold. She came around the car, sat down and turned on the ignition. Then she helped Namita fasten the buckle. "Don't worry if you hear this lemon of mine farting like an old horse," she said, "needs a new muffler, maybe next month when I get my overtime cheque, and sometimes you can smell its fart too, some oil leak somewhere, but I can't afford to fix that yet."

They drove along, Krista continuing her cheerful monologue punctuated with belly laughs. She talked about her grandfather's place in Gimli, her dad's farm in Carmen, and chickens and horses and wheat. Namita felt good listening to her voice. Though she had grown up speaking English at the Christian missionaries' school, Krista's words did not always make sense, with their unfamiliar Canadian accent. Since her arrival, Namita had not met anyone other than her in-laws, and though the television was on all day, she still had not gotten used to the accent and pronunciation of the English spoken in this country. But the laugh was wonderful. In these four months, Namita had not heard anyone laugh a real laugh. Menka, Tarun's brother's wife, laughed often but it was an artificial laugh, a snicker, an ego-filled smirk. The others did not laugh at all, and she had thought she had come to a country where no one laughed, maybe laughing was not even allowed. But Krista laughed, laughed often and loudly. It was so wonderful to hear her, so heartwarming.

"Okay, this is Corydon Avenue, and by the time we come back these cafés will be full of people. Real lively place they've made this strip in the last few years. Girl, as soon as you get yourself a bus pass, and remember that you are entitled to one, just take a bus, any bus, all day, every day, and see our bejesus beautiful city. Say what anyone may about Winterpeg, we have the best transit system in the country, and I suggest you use it like nobody's business because you don't have to think twice about getting into any bus you want as long as you know which bus to take back home. Or rather, as long as you know you should ask the driver for help as soon as you get in. Yes, girl, you'll soon have a home of your own. Once the long weekend is over, we'll get you started on all the paperwork, then you can find out where to get your pass and how to get your résumé ready and soon enough you'll be on your feet, trust me, girl, you *will* be on your feet."

Namita saw that the awnings and café tables ended at an intersection at which stood a large church, so like the churches back home, and then the road went on and on, and Krista bubbled on about how Namita would be taken care of and about women's shelters and welfare forms, and ESL classes, "Though you speak English well enough and wouldn't likely need any," she added and continued talking about provincial assessment of foreign educational transcripts and how there were any number of jobs. "So don't you worry, girl. We'll take care of you."

Then she turned right. "This is Assiniboine Park," she said, "you do know, don't you? that we have three rivers — the Red, the Seine which is a little one, and the Assiniboine. So we have a lot of Assiniboine names around here — Park, Downs, Forest, what have you." She continued to give a guided tour, starting with the Countess of Dufferin, the engine that stood somewhat forlornly on its ancient wheels. As they drove by the Conservatory, Namita sat up when Krista said, "That is where you can see your own tropical trees, girl, you can come again when you have the time, and breathe in the humidity of the rainforest, and do look out for the plaque in honour of my late friend, John Serger, who knew just about everything about every plant anywhere in the world, he was my neighbour and a helpful one too, who gave me one of his rare orchid plants, that I have in my office, come take a look at it some time. And this is the Cricket Pavilion, where, if you come by on a weekend, you can see them playing, mostly they're from Britain and the Caribbean." Namita's eyes brightened and she could imagine a batsman swinging his bat for a boundary to the cheers of a crowd. Then Krista parked the car and they got out.

The sky was so blue, so vast, Namita drew in her breath. "Are you cold?" Krista asked, "Now, if you were like me and had some bum and boobs to speak of, you'd be warmer, I bet," and she opened the car door again and drew out a blanket. "Seems warm enough now but you never know with this bejesus city of ours, even the last week of June can be a dinger. Here, take this. I sure hope old Rufus hasn't been pissing on it; just because he can't see any more, he thinks he can get away with peeing where he pleases," she held it to her nose and said, "No, not since I last washed it, anyway."

"I was just looking at the sky," Namita said, "I've never seen so much blue sky in all my life."

"That's another thing about our old city, girl, say what anyone may, we have skies like nobody's business and it's blue three hundred and forty days a year, even when the thermometer drops to thirty below. So, what's the lowest temperature where you're from?"

Namita smiled shyly. "I don't know. In winter, days sometimes get as cold as it is today, and nights are sometimes... I don't know, like in Jaipur we never keep our eyes and ears on the temperature the way the radio does here every few minutes ..." her voice trailed away with a catch as she thought of home.

Krista was quick to notice the young woman's choking. "Okay, here we go," she started walking at a rapid clip towards the English Garden. When they came to the duck pond, she abruptly sat down on a bench and patted the empty space beside her.

"Girl, you are all out of breath, sit down."

Namita was indeed out of breath, and thankfully sat.

Krista got to her feet almost right away. "I thought your sneakers would help, but I guess you need more time to learn to walk again; that's what abuse does to you, drops you to your knees and you gotta learn all over again to walk. But we'll take care of that, don't you worry. I haven't jogged all week what with all the graveyard overtime and that walk yesterday just wasn't enough, and I'm suffering withdrawal. 'One's gotta to go if one's gotta go'." She laughed. "Just a commercial, don't mind me. Now sit right here and I'll go for my jog, okay?"

Namita nodded. "Okay?" Krista said again.

"Okay," Namita said.

"That's better, see you." And she jogged off.

Namita looked at her as long as she could and then clasped her hands. No, there was no need to be afraid. Yesterday she had panicked, for no reason as it turned out.

*****

Krista had taken her for a walk, during her coffeebreak, and she told the receptionist at the desk, "Just going out for half an hour, to the river, with Namita here, back soon." But when she realized that Namita had a hard time keeping up, she stopped, looked at Namita's sandalled feet and dramatically flung up her arms. "Jesus, girl, your fancy brocade sandals ain't no walking shoes. You just sit here till I get some oxygen into my lungs okay? I'm just taking a short fast walk, okay? Won't be long." They were in a small playground.

There were two children playing in the sandbox, while the two mothers sat on the swing and chatted with each other. Two older children turned up, and so the young women got off the swings and perched themselves on either end of the seesaw. Namita marvelled at the children's hair that seemed to change colour depending on the angle at which the sun shone on them; two were redheads and the other two were blonde. How soft their golden hair seemed, sometimes almost as though they didn't have any, sometimes it shone like hay in the sun. The two little ones were so chubby and the two older ones so confident, like the world was theirs for the taking. The world was so beautiful, waiting to be enjoyed. Maybe, Tarun would appear through the revolving wicket that protected this children's enclosure from the rest of the world, and say it was all a mistake, and he would take her home. After all he hadn't been home the last few days, and would have known only now what his parents and brother had done to her. She stared at the gate till her eyes streamed with the strain.

Then Namita panicked. Krista seemed to have vanished. Namita didn't have a clue where this park was with reference to Bournedaya House, and she thought she could not ask anyone because that is the first thing she had been told — no one outside the women's shelter knew where it was because that is the only way women who came there could be really safe. So maybe she could not let on that Bournedaya House was within a short walking distance of where she was. But if anyone got really lost, she had been told, they could always phone the crisis line, and she had been given a piece of lined paper with the phone number. But she had crushed the paper and thrown it away.

Menka had given her a similar piece of paper with phone numbers, was it only twenty-four hours ago? Menka was married to Tarun's older brother, Bhaiyan. In the afternoon, after the parents-in-law had retired for their nap as though nothing had happened to affect their routine, Menka had come from her bedroom upstairs and sat next to Namita, in the dreary living room with its oversized red sofas and drapes covered with ugly huge flowers. Menka had whispered that there were places Namita could go to, and she had offered her a sheet on which were written words and phone numbers: Immigrant Women's Association of Manitoba, Immigrant Women's Employment Counselling, International Centre, Salvation Army. "Phone one of these," she whispered, "they can help."

Namita was grateful for what she thought was Menka's sudden support.

"Help get him back?" she asked.

Menka smirked. "No, not him, but they can help you survive when you get thrown out. Phone them now, while you have a phone. Here, keep these too," rummaging through her handbag, she thrust four quarters into Namita's palm forcing her hand open. "So you can phone me at this time any day, when they are sleeping," she gestured towards the old couple's room. And then she walked up the stairs to her room. She had a mincing walk, her left hip swayed more than her right, and her silver anklets seductively tinkled. Namita felt goosebumps of fear all over her arms. What did she mean, when she got thrown out?

That morning, at 10:58, as noted on the envelope of papers that still lay on the night table next to her bed, she had been served divorce papers. A delivery person had come to the door. Her father-in-law had greeted him cordially as one would a long-awaited visitor. He took the envelope, sheet and pen that the man handed him, and extending the sheet and pen to Namita, said, "Just sign your name here." Thinking it was a parcel from India, she eagerly took the sheet and signed it. Even as she handed it over to the man, she read the words, "Received a copy of the Petition," and suddenly realized this man was not a mailman, and that these papers held danger. She snatched it back from the man, and ran towards the kitchen. No, she would not sign it. She would not accept the envelope, no matter what it contained, that her father-in-law held in his hand. She stood at the kitchen door, sheet in hand. As long as she did not sign for it, he could not give it to her, whatever it was. "Give it at once." Her father-in-law barked at her. She crumpled the sheet and closed her fist around it. She would not accept whatever it was that they were forcing on her. If they wanted her to have it, it was something bad. But the man left it anyway. Carefully poising a new delivery sheet on his knee, he wrote something, handed it to her father-in-law and left. She stumbled to her room and sat on the bed while Menka and her mother-in-law set about preparing lunch. Her father-in-law came to her room, placed the envelope on the bed next to her, and went out, closing the door behind him.

Namita took out the sheaf of papers from the envelope that her father-in-law had already opened. The top sheet was a copy of what she had crumpled. The courier had written, "REFUSED TO SIGN," and "10:58 am" The cover sheet of the stapled sheaf of papers read *PETITION FOR DIVORCE*.

Everyone went on as though nothing had happened. While she sat on the bed in her room, they had lunch, washed up, and the parents-in-law went to their room for their afternoon nap. She had come out of her room and sat in the living room with its ugly drapes, and Menka had joined her to give the sheet of paper with the phone numbers of the various agencies.

Which is why Namita had crumpled up the memo-sheet with the phone number of Bournedaya House crisis line that the counsellor had given her.

And now, as she sat in the children's playground, she did not know where she was or where she could go or what she should do as she sat on the bench where Krista had left her. One of the children was curious about her and was circling his way towards her, but his mother called him back. No one wanted her, not her husband's family, not these strangers. Only Krista said everything would be taken care of, and Krista had disappeared. Namita sat petrified on the bench, staring and staring at the poplar that was shutting out the sun. A scream was working its way up her throat from the pit of her stomach, but it did not emerge. Instead, she could feel its python coils stretching inside her larynx and choking her. She wanted to scream and scream and get it all out, but no sound came. And then Krista had appeared, her T-shirt all wet with sweat and a big grin on her face. She sat next to Namita, and said, "Jesus, I feel better now, not as good as if I'd really jogged but a fast walk is okay too. I'll get you some walking shoes when we get back."

*****

Krista had got her the cardigan and runners last night, and now here she was in Assiniboine Park, in someone else's shoes. Surely surely they were not hers for long; Tarun would find her and ask her to throw back these unsightly clothes that Krista had fished for her from a closet in the counsellors' room and he would take her back home.

Namita pulled the cardigan closer around herself on feeling a sudden breeze. The cardigan was too big, and she had rolled up the sleeves four inches; the base colour was a dull grey, but there were Fair-Isle patterns and bright geometric diamonds of blue and a red line running through the diamond. Namita looked down at her legs. Krista called these pants *sweatpants*, and they were just like Krista's, fleecy navy-coloured pull-ons.

On the duck pond, there were no birds. Some children on parent's leash peered in, looking for fish, and then they went away, parent and children pretending to chase each other. Soon after, four birds flew in and circled overhead, flapping their brown wings as they came down in a slow spiral. They landed on the surface of the pond, and suddenly they were not brown any more. Bright turquoise lined their back between the brown, and on either side of the neck flashed a brilliant patch of peacock blue. And now their heads were green, now dark blue. They floated without disturbing the surface, as though they were part of a still life painting. And then some children ran towards the water, parents in tow, wanting to feed popcorn to the birds, which paddled away to the farther end of the pond.

Peacock blue. Namita's memory raced home to Jaipur.

*****

Not far from the gates of her father's house was a place they called the peacock garden. It was on an estate owned by Seth Govind Das, with a house recessed on the far side. A wicket gate allowed public access to the private garden. At the centre was a shallow pond, fed by rain water, that was often dry. Radiating from it were paths of fine golden sand that shimmered like waves when the sun was blazing, but in the morning and late afternoon the sand was fine and cool under their bare feet. Along the path that led to the house at the far end were tall Ashoka trees, their slender trunks and tapering conical shapes reaching upwards. The other paths had flowering trees, bougainvillae of deep pink, great big gulmohurs with their flaming orange-red flowers. Closer to the house were creepers of jasmine and raat-ki-rani and chameli, their delicate fragrance welcoming visitors into the private compound of the house. The estate was surrounded by a hedge of thorny keekar and cactus-like bushes that kept cattle from entering the garden. They stretched their twisted branches in different directions, the white naag-champa nodding on the twisted branches like the hood of a snake.

At one end of the garden was an enclosure of mesh. Inside were four peacocks and as many peahens. This was a favourite haunt for the children in the neighbourhood. They spent hours watching the birds. These peacocks seemed to open their fans every time their master came near the enclosure. At other times they would strut their fan on whim.

Namita and her sister Asha, and later her brothers as well, would stand entranced, watching the birds lazily drawing their long brown tails behind them, the feathers all bunched together so that the bright eyes on their tails did not stand out. Then one would stop, turn around once or twice, and twitch his tail and slowly lift it, spreading his fan in a glorious circle of swirling blue and green and purple. He would solemnly move towards a peahen, and stand still. Or he would come close to the children and slant his head sideways. Sometimes, the peacocks would suddenly close their fan and run, their raucous shrill cry scaring the wits out of the children. It happened everytime, the chill of fear when that raucous cry split their ears.

Seth Govind Das had another obsession as well. He had statues of Lord Krishna all over the garden. Of different kinds and sizes. Of stone and wood and terra cotta and ceramic. In different poses, but the majority standing in the familiar pose of crossed feet, flute at mouth. Some were broken at the edges, some worn flat as though dredged from the bottom of the sea. Many were crude, made by stonecutters rather than sculptors, but the old man bought any statue anyone brought to his door. He fed these artists, even if they only pretended to be one so they could get access to his legendary hospitality and stay a few weeks chipping at large rocks on his estate.

At the far end of the garden was his house, separated from the public section by a three-foot high hedge of green. Along the verandahs and in the small front courtyard were the more artistic ones, and only special neighbours were invited into this part. Namita's family was special. Their mother often sent, through the children, special delicacies and festival sweets for the old man. He had no family with him who could provide the kind of home-cooked food their mother could. Their mother also sent him a bowl of whatever special offering she made everyday to God in her pooja room. He, in turn, would give them dried fruits and flowers to take back to their mother. He loved children, especially Namita and her siblings, whom he saw every day, unlike his grandchildren who came for short visits, never long enough for them to be at ease with him.

He lived alone, with a houseful of retainers who cooked and cleaned and spent their days tending the garden. His grown sons and daughters lived in Delhi, where they had a family business. During the winter months, they periodically drove down with their entourage, stayed a day or two at a time, and went back.

One day, when Namita and Asha excitedly told him about the upcoming wedding of a schoolmate's older sister, he told them that when they got married, he would give each of them the statue of their choice. Close to the front door of his house was a Krishna of black granite, exquisitely chiselled, almost life-size. Namita pointed to the granite Krishna that was clearly the old man's most treasured piece, and laughingly said, "Even that one? Will you give me even that one, if I choose?" and he said, "Certainly, as long as you promise you will carry it away carefully to your husband's house."

It was a conversation they repeated and shared. But one day, Namita decided to be smart. Even at that age, she was more practical than Asha, and had figured out a bird in hand was worth two in the bush.

"Why don't I just take a baby Krishna now instead of the big one later?" and he had said, "Fair enough," and she had chosen a wooden Krishna about twelve inches high. For months she had carried it around, dressed it and fed it, pretending she was Princess Meera, who had carried around just such a statue and had become Lord Krishna's favourite friend so that he came whenever she called him. Then she had stood it on a table in her room, and she could see it even now as she sat near the duck pond here in distant Winnipeg.

Now, she thought longingly of that statue. Bina-Ma would be taking good care of it, she knew.

Bina-Ma. Namita sighed. How far away she was from Bina-Ma, mother who was not her mother and yet more than mother.

Namita was six and Asha eight when their mother started dying. She took a long time to die. There were months of intense pain, followed by months of remission. The girls were old enough to feel the stress, and they walked on tiptoe and spoke in whispers even when Mother was well enough to do all the usual chores of braiding their hair, serving Papaji's breakfast, lunch and dinner, and overseeing the housework done by two different maids who came at different times so that at least one was around at any given time. She died two months after Asha had got her first period. It was as though she had kept herself alive to see her daughter through that step. "You have to tell all that I tell you now to Namita when her time comes," she had said.

But Asha did not have to. Their father got married again six months later.

Suddenly home was bright and cheerful again. Bina was only eight years older than Asha, and so they worked out a compromise to add Ma to her name instead of calling her by her name or calling her Ma or Chhoti Ma (Little Mother). Bina was a strong young woman, with strong hands, big white teeth, high jawbones and a laugh that made the girls' world bright. They went off to the bazaar every weekend, and bought all kinds of ribbons and hair clips and beads and bangles over which they played and quarrelled together. Though Bina-Ma did not join in their skipping rope games, for she got pregnant within months of arriving, she would play every other game with them and their friends.

Soon after Papaji brought Bina home, whenever the girls visited neighbours or relatives, they would have commiseration and pity poured on them for being motherless and orphaned, and they would have to listen to more covert hints by the well-meaning nosy-pokes of how sad it was that Father had re-married before the poor woman's ashes had got cold. Then Asha and Namita would come home and mimic what they had been told to Bina-Ma and all three would laugh and laugh till their stomachs hurt.

But Bina-Ma was Mother too. She kept the house clean and tidy at all times, and trained the girls in kitchen work. She arranged for a music Master to come and give them singing lessons, and made them teach her the songs after the Master left, even though she had a tone-deaf ear that could not pick up any nuances. She packed off the cook and taught the girls to help her in the kitchen every day. She was always laughing but she had all of them, including Papaji, under her thumb. Very soon, two brothers, Akhil and Nikhil, appeared. Over the next few years, the girls doted on the little boys and they in return worshipped their sisters. Even as toddlers, they knew when to expect the girls home from school, and they'd be all ready and impatient to be taken out for a walk to Sethji's peacock garden. Sethji loved all of them, and whenever he was not busy with something else, he would carry the baby, hold the other by hand, and all of them would walk to the peacocks and watch the proud display.

*****

Namita could see the peacocks in these small birds in front of her, the cerulean blue darting from their necks as they floated by with little movements of neck and webbed feet.

If she were to ask Krista to let her phone Jaipur, Bina-Ma would arrange for her flight home; she was sure of that, though she knew her father had already dipped into his retirement fund in order to buy her the ticket the first time. There had been talk about how it was almost as cheap to buy a return flight as a one-way flight, but Bina-Ma had been against it; a bride who was on her way to live with her husband should not have a return ticket. Bina didn't want to say aloud that it was a bad omen. Instead she said that girls should know that their new home was where they belonged.

Yes, Bina-Ma would sell her own bangles if need be to arrange for a ticket. But no, Namita would not ask. Surely Tarun would come around, surely all this was a mistake, and the only way she could make sure it was a mistake was to stay right here and wait for Tarun.

Tarun would never have allowed what had happened to happen. Around three o'clock, after the nap which the others had taken as though nothing out of the ordinary had happened, Menka and her father-in-law had come into her room and asked her to pack. They had brought in her empty second suitcase, which had been stowed in the basement, and they had opened the closet doors and told her to pack her things. She had started crying. They then shut the door on her and went to have their afternoon tea and snacks.

In the closet was a locked Samsonite suitcase, given as part of her trousseau, in which most of the elaborately embroidered salwar suits and saris still lay untouched. There had been no occasion to wear any of them. Her mother-in-law went out with her husband for a walk every day after their afternoon tea, and Menka and Bhaiyan often went out late evenings, but Namita was kept secluded. From her Samsonite suitcase, she had taken out a couple of silk saris, her favourite parrot-green Banarsi silk, and blue Conjeevaram, and worn them in the evenings before Tarun's return from work. These saris and other artificial silks hung in the closet. Her everyday salwar suits lay folded on closet shelves. Namita closed the closet door, sat on her bed and cried.

She cried all the way to dinnertime; her mother-in-law came in and said, "Please don't cry, please don't cry, you are making me feel so sorry, please." Then her father-in-law had dragged his wife away forcibly, had come back and bellowed, "Can't you see how you are making poor Ma-ji ill? Get going, quick!"

She continued to cry, and Menka came in and threw all her saris and suits into the suitcase. When she came to the parrot-green sari that Namita had worn for the wedding reception, Menka held it up and said, "This is Tarun's favourite colour, maybe I'll keep it safe for you." Namita hurled herself against the other woman.

At the wedding reception, as they had sat on bedecked throne-like chairs side by side, Tarun had told her about how coincidental it was that she had chosen his favourite colour, and she had thought it a good omen, that they would be in synch forever and forever.

"Don't you dare, don't you dare touch my sari," Namita clawed at Menka in unbridled grief, and snatched it back. Menka turned away with a shrug. "Who cares? You can keep all your saris, not that I can see any use for them where you are going to be. You keep your saris, and I'll keep your ..." she drawled, leaving her sentence unfinished.

Menka was like that, full of innuendoes. Over the last four months, she had needled Namita with subtle and not-so-subtle hints about Tarun's eyes and hands that couldn't keep away from nice-looking women; and why not, she had said quite openly, who would want a featherless crow when one could have a cute *koel*? Menka was proud of her looks, her little turned up nose and chubby face with deep dimples on both cheeks, and she thought Namita plain. Often she would dismiss Namita's choice of sari colours, drawling that the colour itself was lovely but surely Namita knew it was not right for her.... These exchanges always took place in the living room, after the in-laws had retired for their nap. Namita could never figure out just what Menka had implied until afterwards, when she thought back over the exchanges. The words were always double-edged; they implied that it was well-known around town that Tarun was a flirt; or that Menka and Tarun had a relationship that was special, that she came first at all times and would for all time, and that she, Menka, was the only woman in Tarun's life.

Namita brooded over these exchanges, had tried to give excuses for her husband at every turn — he liked to enjoy life, have a drink and a cigarette when he came home, he was just being more free with Menka because he knew her better, she having come to Winnipeg a whole year earlier than Namita. Most of all, he was being pressured by his family to keep away from his wife, and so could not show her any affection as long as his parents were around. That was it. His family. Once he got out of their clutches, he would be all right; meanwhile, if he chose to flirt with his sister-in-law, well, it would pass. He would come around. It was only a matter of time. She would be patient. With these and similar rationalizings, she had explained away so many things that seemed beyond her.

Their living arrangements had upset her, but she knew the reason why her in-laws were so against her, and was willing to wait. While Bhaiyan and Menka, had the master bedroom that occupied the entire upstairs of the one and a half storey house, and his parents had their bedroom on the ground floor, she and Tarun had only a small room with a single bed. Tarun kept his clothes and books in another small room at the back. He always went out after dinner and came back very late. Quickly, furtively, he would slide into her bed, make love and leave for his couch in the living room. Very often, he was away for a couple of days; it was his work, he said, he had to be on the road a lot. She had realized that his salary of $1,500 a month was far from a princely sum in Canada. She suspected that he was doing some very menial job that he did not want to talk about. But she had accepted that. One had to start on the lowest rung of the ladder and work one's way up. As she was willing to, in her climb into her in-laws' hearts.

There were many things she could not understand about her new family. But she had thought she would be accepted one day, once they got over the wrangle about her dowry. And then had come the divorce papers. Go back, they had said, go back the way you came here. Since you didn't wait for your husband to send you a ticket, you can go back on your own.

*****

She would stay on in Winnipeg. Girls should know that their new home was where they belonged.

Krista was back. They sat side by side on the bench for a few minutes. Then Krista rose with her usual "Let's get the work done" efficiency and led the way to the car.

"Let's take another route going back," she said. "You've got to see where the *beautiful people* live." She slowly drove along the road between vast stretches of grass where a great many people in colourful shorts and T-shirts were walking with children or by themselves. These were beautiful people. Indeed, Namita had never seen so much of bare skin among people of her own class. Peasants and working class men back home wore hardly anything. But the women here were just as bare and so beautiful, it took her breath away. But then, everything was taking her breath away. It was all so new, all so wonderful, and Krista was the most wonderful of all, large-hearted Krista sitting by her and bubbling away about Wellington Crescent houses as they drove out through the park gates. As they slowly drove past the manorial houses, Namita realized what Krista meant by *beautiful people*.

"Look to your left," Krista said, breaking into Namita's thoughts, "ain't that a beauty or what? One day, girl, you and me'll buy it, what says you?" Namita looked at the house — it was something vaguely familiar, that she had grown up with, but she couldn't place it immediately — the brownstone, the castle-like square tops and gables, the narrow vertical windows in walls speckled with stone projections, the high wrought-iron gates.

"Shakespeare," she said, pleased that it had come to her. "Shakespeare's England," she saw the old school textsbooks that her father had used in his school days, and that she had read when she was in high school with such delight to her little brothers even though their vocabulary was all of twenty words.

"What are you talking about, girl? Where did you read about Shakespeare and all?"

"In high school and college, doesn't everyone?"

Krista whistled. This young woman knew Shakespeare. She should be okay soon, then. On first seeing her, Krista had thought she would be totally helpless, with her outlandish clothes, heavy gold jewellery and silver-work sandals, but if she knew Shakespeare, and since she spoke English well, she'd be okay. Krista wondered about this young woman, rather different from most others who had come to their doorstep. She had been at the desk when the call came through, first from the Salvation Army crisis line and then from the young woman herself. A garbled story, full of sobs and pauses, saying she had nowhere to go, her family had thrown her out (at which there were voices in the background shushing her up), she was a new immigrant, and had got their phone number from the Salvation Army Crisis Line. Krista had asked for the address so she could send a taxi, and again there were voices in the background and then Namita had answered that she'd be at the Circle K store at the corner of Leila and McPhillips.

Which is where Namita's brother-in-law had deposited her. He had sat in his car until the taxi came and then he had taken off.

Krista had tried to trace the call, but it had been blocked. She realized that she was dealing with shifty people who thought they knew the rules and how to break them with impunity.

Now, as they drove over Maryland Bridge, she said, "Girl, those men in your family, they're devils incarnate, they blocked their number before they made you call, didn't they?"

Namita said she did not know what that meant. "Never mind," Krista said, "never you mind, you'll be okay."

Namita thought of how she had been forced to make the call to Bournedaya House. Her father-in-law and brother-in-law had stood over her and told her to phone the Salvation Army crisis line, and she had resisted them for an hour, crying in a wild paroxysm that kept them away, but the moment her paroxysm had spent itself, they had literally twisted her arm, had dialled the Salvation Army number, and had listened in on the cordless extension while she was given the Bournedaya House telephone number. They had then told her to dial that number, and she had refused. They had left her alone for a while. Even in all the trauma of the situation, she had figured out that if she did not speak, they might be at a loss as to what to do next; not that it had prevented the delivery of the *Petition for Divorce*. But clearly her resistance did mean something, so she resisted. Meanwhile it was getting dark. Even the long June day had to end.

Then the two men stood over her as she cowered on the ugly

red sofa. They told her she did not know the laws of this land; that if they were to phone the police and complain that she was an intruder, an illegal alien, the police would take her away, lock her up, send her back to where she came from. To Gehunnum, they added, because that was where she belonged, in hell. They had her passport, all the papers concerning her education, her Fine Arts degree, and she could dance herself lame. But if she behaved herself, she could take everything she had brought with her, passport, saris and all. They did not mention her jewellery, which they had appropriated soon after the wedding.

Even in her wild grief and helplessness, she had figured out they had a trump card — the threat of deportation; if the police got her, she would never see Tarun again. She had to be in Winnipeg, when Tarun came back from wherever he was. He would come back.

So she had asked for her passport. "Don't you trust us, you bitch?" her brother-in-law had said. No, she wanted to say, never. But she had only repeated, "Give me my passport," and they had given it to her. Then she had let them dial Bournedaya House.

*****

Krista parked her car on the road in front of Bournedaya House instead of in the parking lot. "I'll see you to the lounge and then take off," she said.

When they entered the foyer, the receptionist got up and ran over, "Thank God you're here, Krista, do we ever need you. Alina is back, and pregnant too."

Krista rushed to the anteroom, forgetting all about Namita, who followed her.

Alina was half reclining on the four-seater sofa. Her arm was bandaged in blood-soaked segments of a bed sheet, her left eye hidden in a monstrous swelling and she lay with the other eye open, watching her children. They seemed to be about ages three and five. They stood on either side of her knees, staring at her solemnly with big dark eyes. Brown hair was tightly curled on their heads. They were beautiful little children, their skin a smooth chocolate brown, their eyes solemn.

Krista dropped to her knees and gathered them up. "My, my, my," she said, "I am so glad to have you back. I've missed you guys like nobody's business. Your Royal Highness Robby, and Your Royal Highness Deena? Come, come, do you remember your own little room from before? The one with little birdies on the drapes?"

Their solemn eyes turned to her and then they smiled, the smile working slowly down to their mouths. They closed their eyes, and murmured against her breast, as children do when they are safely cuddled.

"He was laid off," Alina said. "It's not his fault. A man who cannot feed his family gets broken."

"And so he breaks his wife's bones?" Krista said.

"He is a good man," Alina said stubbornly.

Krista released the children, and said softly, "Now my most favourite little Robby and Deena are going to have something to eat before they go to bed, right? Joan will help you choose what you want. Go with her while I take care of Mama."

They turned their eyes to their mother again, and leaned over her knees. They would not leave her. Krista cradled them again, crooning them to safety.

Namita went to her room, sat on her bed, and cried as she had never cried before. Then she curled herself into as small a figure as she could and cried into her pillow.

Krista came in at some point. She sat on the empty bed next to Namita's, and said, "Come, girl, if you want to go to bed without supper, go ahead, but the least you could do is get under the covers, right?" Namita pulled herself up and flung her arms around Krista. How soft her bosom was, and how gentle her hands. Namita remembered the times she nestled into Bina-Ma's blouse, always wet with milk, with the sour-sweetness of milk that had dried on the bodice. Bina-Ma nursed her children into their second year, and even longer for the older one, who was jealous if he could not get to her the same time his brother did.

Krista allowed her to take comfort. "Makes me feel almost guilty when I go home to my family," she said. "And you can take heart, I guess, that you haven't been beaten black and blue."

Krista waited. This young woman should bounce back sooner

than most, she thought. It was something about her, her sense of wonder at this new world. It would be so good, she thought, if this young woman would come back and help out once she was on her feet. But she would not hold her breath on that. These Asian women, they were a secretive bunch; never wanted to let on they had ever been in a shelter, or on welfare. Something about their culture, she supposed, that made them disappear the moment they had been helped to their feet. Never wanted to recognize each other, either, like Farzana who had vanished from the lounge on seeing that Namita too was brown skinned, like her. If these women would just realize they didn't have to feel ashamed simply because their partners were devil's own double-dyed jerks, if they would just recognize each other and share their stories, if they could just spread the word that there was help available and no woman need put up with shit.... No, the few Asian women who did find their way here vanished as soon as they could and never came back, or never even sent an anonymous thank you card. Never mind, as long as they got back on their feet, Krista thought, always generous in her reactions.

Chapter Two

The next morning, Namita was told she had been assigned a counsellor from the Immigrant Women's Association of Manitoba, who would soon visit her. She sat in the lounge all morning, waiting for her.

Shayna was quite unlike Krista, but she was caring and supportive in her own quiet way. A small-made woman in her forties, she spoke slowly and softly in measured voice and tone. She took down a great many routine details of Namita's background: when and where she was married, when she had got her sponsorship papers, when she had arrived. She scanned the divorce papers, and said, "Have you gone through these? Don't worry, you don't need to. I think the first thing we have to do is to get you a Legal Aid lawyer. Once the long weekend is over, we can get started. I'll arrange that you continue to stay here for a few days."

In the lunch room was a large notice, asking everyone to be there at three o'clock to listen to an announcement by Krista. While the others went their ways after lunch, Namita stayed on, counting the minutes to three o'clock when she could see Krista's friendly face again and talk about her morning meeting with Shayna.

Krista came in at exactly three o'clock, a tornado of energy. She greeted everyone by name, held Robby and Deena by hand, and announced that everyone who wished to would go to the Forks at eight o'clock and stay for the fireworks. Seeing Namita's surprised look, she turned to Robby and said, "My little Superman, do you think you could explain to this young lady what we are celebrating?" Solemnly, he whispered, "Canada Day."

"And what is that?"

"Canada's birthday," piped in a happier child. "Birthday candles, birthday cake."

"Right-oh, and songs and fireworks, eeoo." The children in the room got excited. Their mothers smiled wanly. Counsellors got everyone to join hands, and they danced in and out, side to side, any way they chose, pulling and pushing the circle in different directions.

*****

That evening, there were several new people, men and women, waiting to take them out to the Forks. "Where's everyone?" Krista boomed. There weren't too many residents assembled. Robby and Deena were in Joan's care without their mother, but Krista felt there should be more. Over the intercom, she boomed, "Okay people, you have a choice: you can mope in the corner of your room, you can watch a show on TV or you can come with us and join some real fun."

In the next few minutes, a few more women appeared. Krista talked about what they would do, who was in charge of whom, who was to hold whose hand and never let go, and she introduced the new volunteers. "Say what anyone may," she boomed, "our Winterpeg is the world's volunteerism capital, as you can see. Let's give them a big hand." The women clapped half-heartedly.

But when the evening was over one of the women thanked the volunteers and there were hugs and handshakes all around, and the clapping went on and on, waking some of the children, who were crooned back to sleep. Rick, one of the volunteers, sat on a sofa, holding sleeping Robby and Deena on his lap while waiting for someone to take them to their room.

The receptionist came to Namita and said Tarun had called earlier saying he would call again, that she should wait for his call and not do anything till then. A great load lifted from her heart. Tarun was back. All would be well. He would clear up all this terrible nightmare. She quickly deciphered his message to mean that he knew everything that had happened but, as he was still under his family's control, she should not call him at his parent's home, but just wait for him to contact her. She was relieved. She understood it perfectly. She would be patient.

Her first Canada Day in this country had turned out to be a real birthday party, after all. The world was a safe place, just as it had been in the days of Bhagavan Rama.

*****

Namita remembered her childhood winter evenings, when Akhil and Nikhil were babies, as her most treasured memories. During the day, cooking was done on the gas and electric stoves on the cooking table. In the evenings, Bina-Ma had two coal *sigris* lit by the maid before she left; well before the time Papaji usually returned from work. She would put the dahl-pot on one coal-stove and the vegetable skillet on the other. Both would cook on the very slow heat for as long as the children needed to play with their dad, or do their homework. When it was time for dinner, she would sit on the wooden *paat* on the floor next to the sigris, take down the vegetable skillet and replace it with the chappati skillet, and start rolling out the dough that the maid had kneaded and covered. The girls would set out the plates, stainless steel tumblers of water, *paats* to sit on, and clap a spoon on a plate to call the men-folk and Papaji would come in, carrying Nikhil while Akhil hung around his knees, and all would sit in a circle around the warm sigri.

Bina-Ma would serve them hot chappatis, thin and soft, topped with ghee, and they would eat and chat, chat and eat. After everything was put away, they would continue to sit around the warm sigris, now with no pot on them and the coal almost spent. The girls would sit on either side of Bina-Ma, leaning into her, and the boys would be on their father's lap. Then Bina-Ma would open her

Ramayana and tell them a story each day. Her volume had many coloured pictures. The girls would open the book to where the tassel bookmark was in main narrative of the epic, so they could start each evening where they had left off the previous evening.

Bina-Ma never read from the book. Rather she would tell the stories from memory, with her own digressions, and always find place to insert something about Papaji; every good quality any hero or heroine had in the story came right around to Papaji. The girls were old enough to recognize in some way that Bina-Ma's interpolations were naughty, and referred to something that happened between their parents in private moments. It gave them great joy to know that they were part of whatever it was that was happening between their parents around the warm sigri, while the boys slept in their father's arms, and the colours jumped off the book's pages in their mother's lap and Bhagavan Ramachandra and his happy monkey-friends marched onward toward Lanka so that the world could be a safe place for everyone.

*****

Two days went by, and Tarun still had not called. Many places were closed for the long weekend. Namita had stayed in the whole time, to be sure she was there for the telephone call. Tuesday morning, newspaper on her lap, she was calm. Her in-laws being what they were, she could imagine what had happened. Tarun would have been out-talked, and they would have brought up the whole wrangle over her dowry.

*****

Papaji was an austere man in some ways. He belonged to a group led by a progressive swami who advocated a simple life of honesty and hard work. No smoking, no drinking, no eating meat, no dishonest deals in business or in personal life. Big deal, Bina-Ma would say dismissively of all the forbidden pleasures, Who has the time or money for all that anyway?

When Asha turned eighteen, marriage talks became the main

conversation at dinner every evening. Papaji always started off with his dictum of refusing any prospective alliances which did not meet his "No smoking, no drinking, no eating meat , no dowry" criteria, and Bina-Ma would intervene along the lines of, "He has to be almost as handsome as Papaji, because no one can be more good-looking ..." and look with dancing eyes at her husband. Bina-Ma had a way of flirting with him in the presence of the girls because they had been there from her day one, and she had figured she'd make it part of the family's togetherness.

Within six months, they had a match, a perfect match, so the astrologers maintained. The young man was an engineer, the eldest son of Seth Pratap, who came from an old Jaipur family. They lived at the other end of the city, but it was a comfort that their Asha would be in the city of her birth after all.

The families met several times. Once, they visited at Bina-Ma's invitation. Papaji was dead set against such an occasion saying he would have none of anything that bore even a whiff of dowry negotiations, but Bina-Ma had her way. It is best to talk about their expectations face to face, she said. She wanted to show them the jewellery Asha would be getting, and that would open up conversation about what else they expected. She did not use the tabooed word, dowry.

So there they were one Wednesday afternoon, Seth Pratap and his wife, and a sister of hers. After hot pakoras stuffed with choice cashews, and steaming hot jalebis, and masala tea, the men sat on chairs and talked whatever men talk about, and the women sat on a silk mat, where Bina-Ma had spread out the jewellery. The jewellery sets lay in two large trays, in open velvet-lined boxes. There were three complete sets of necklace, earrings and bangles on each tray, and several single pieces of gold chain, pendants and bracelets. She explained that this was the jewellery left by the girls' mother, "may her soul be at peace", all the jewellery she had owned, she said that several times so it would sink in that she was not keeping any for herself. She had made it into two equal halves, one for each of the girls. Asha's parents-in-law could choose which half they wanted, though she herself favoured the one with the jade set because jade was Asha's lucky stone.

At this point, Seth Pratap dragged his chair towards the women, and leaned forward. He carefully picked up the jade set and placed it on the coffee table next to his chair. "Exquisite, exquisite," he said, "and all the more dear for having been worn by a good woman, may her soul be at peace. Chand Sahab, it is a good omen indeed because jade is my family's lucky stone as well, and I insist on giving our daughter-in-law a jade set on her wedding day. For, let me be frank with my fears, Chand Sahab, jade is a 'nakhra' gem, a whimsical stone, and its flaws latch on to the wearer. We have a family jeweller who is the best connoisseur of jade Jaipur has ever known, and we shall pick perfect flawless gems, be sure of that. Not that I mean to say anything less than the best about this blessed lady's perfect set, Chand Sahab, but I have taken a vow that we shall give a jade set to each daughter-in-law who enters our home. And so," he put the jade set on the farther tray that Bina-Ma had assigned for Namita and transferred a ruby set from it to the tray to his left, meant for Asha.

"Very generous of you, Pratap Sahab, very generous, my daughter is lucky indeed to be getting a jade set from you."

"Not at all, Chand Sahab, all of us want our children's happiness do we not? And now," (he said the *now* with a deliberate pause as though to say "Listen") he took a pearl set from the Namita's tray and exchanged it with an amethyst set on Asha's. "Pearls and rubies go well together. This way, our dear Asha can mix and match the two sets."

"Of course, of course, excellent taste, Seth Sahab."

Soon both trays were on the coffeetable. One by one, Seth Pratap picked up the jewellery and if he made an exchange, he gave a very beautifully worded explanation to which Papaji gladly nodded acquiescence. He surveyed the new arrangement and stretched it towards the ladies so they could admire his choice.

"And now," he turned to Papaji, "Chand Sahab, you are a sharif (honourable) person, as all of Jaipur knows, and so I can say this to you without being misunderstood. Your late blessed wife, may whose soul be at peace, has given much. And it is right that you share it between your daughters equally. But have you considered this? That maybe you could give each of them a complete set of her jewellery, half that were worn by her and the other half that are replicas of the rest? Think how happy it would make each of your lovely daughters, to have a complete set of their dear mother's jewellery. Now, my family jeweller has the best workers in all of Jaipur, and he can make a duplicate set perfect in every detail."

From the cloth bag he had brought, he extracted mesh bags, one red and the other green. The girls watched from the doorway, fascinated that he should have exactly what he wanted in his bag. He carefully slid each tray into one of the bags, which being fine mesh, enlarged just enough to cover it snugly. "So here it is, behn-ji," he gestured to Bina-Ma to take them away. "The red bag is our daughter's blessed mother's jewellery, and in the green one are the pieces which our jeweller will duplicate for you so you can add them to our daughter's. My jeweller has his own stamp which he imprints on the back of every piece he makes, and so you will have no trouble figuring out which is the original and which the new piece. I'll phone our jeweller tomorrow and we can fix up a time to visit his shop. I will myself drive you there, Chand Sahab, and of course Behn-ji too if she so wishes."

"Of course, of course," Papaji said. "Very kind of you, sir, very kind indeed."

"Now, one more detail, if I may, Chand Sahab, for you are a sharif man and will listen patiently. Over the past decades, I have gone to numberless marriages in my extended family, but this is to be the first in my own house. I would very much want everyone, no matter how far away they are, to attend this happy occasion. So sending them tickets would help, don't you think? Not airfare or anything like that. Just first class train fare would do."

"Of course, of course," Papaji said.

"Now, let us see. Twenty thousand cash should do, I think. I will take care of any extra that might be needed. Twenty thousand?"

"Certainly, no problem," Papaji said.

*****

When Papaji returned from the gate after seeing them off,

Bina-Ma was in a classic pose of mockery — finger on cheek, rolling eyes — and the girls were holding their sides laughing.

"Quiet. What have I got myself into? If that wasn't a dowry-session, what was it? It is all your fault."

Bina-Ma laughed it away. "Don't fret so much, Chand Sahab, I know you are a sharif person." And all three young women laughed and laughed till their stomachs hurt. But Bina-Ma pulled short, and said in a serious voice, "Don't fret. I told you it is best to be upfront about it. After all, dowry is just the old way of making sure daughters also, and not just the sons, get a share of their father's property."

"Old ways have to change, dowry is illegal, and I'll be damned if I marry my daughter to anyone barbaric enough to demand dowry."

"Shh. They are nice people, believe me, they are. I can feel it. He is an astute businessman, but an honest one. He'll keep his side of the deal, believe me Asha has a happy life ahead."

That night, when the boys were in bed, and Papaji in his recliner, they laughed all over again as Bina-Ma told them of Pratap Sahab's brilliant sleight-of-hand. She herself had halved the share by ensuring that the overall weight of gold in each half was about the same, but Pratap Sahab had rearranged Asha's share of her mother's jewellery so that it was much heavier than the other half; and since his own jeweller was going to replicate the rest, the Seth would make sure the gold in the new jewellery would be much more than in her mother's. Smart man, beti, smart family you are getting into.

Papaji, who thought he would pretend he did not hear, was needled into entering the conversation. "And where do you think the money for all the extra gold and stones is to come from?"

"Not from a class-two civil servant's salary, for sure," Bina-Ma laughed. "The girls' mother, good woman, seems to have managed the house far better than I, that she saved enough from your civil servant's salary to build up a nest-egg."

"She came with all that jewellery," Papaji said gruffly, remembering how little he had given her of gifts or time.

"I don't mean that, but this," and Bina-Ma opened the little pouch that always hung from her waist, and let two balls of raw gold peek out. "Aren't you glad I didn't show them these, else he would have talked you out of these two nuggets as well. I don't know if there is enough gold here to make a complete set. You'll just have to dip into your Provident Fund ..."

"My Provident Fund is just that — for our retirement, and not to be frittered away on dowry" — he spat out the forbidden word. "Thank God we need to make only Asha's half now."

"Oh, no," Bina-Ma said, "we have to make both at the same time. Both girls must have an equal share. And moreover, Asha's part of her mother's treasures will go with her and we'll forget what their patterns are by the time our little Namita gets married. Chand Sahab, sharif Chand Sahab, you will just have to borrow the money from somewhere. But believe me, Asha will be happy."

And indeed she was. Asha's in-laws were good people, and they treated her with love. And she did her part too. She took over a great many responsibilities from her mother-in-law without ever making her feel she was not every bit a good mistress of the house and the tyrannical mother-in-law she was expected to be. Within three years, she bore two children in the right order, first a son and then a daughter, and everyone approved her every step. Except Papaji. When she became pregnant within six months of the wedding, he swore he wouldn't get Namita married off until she was twenty-one. "It was different with us," he said, knowing his women would start a spell of laughter, "If we had waited, why, Asha might have ended up with a brother young enough to be her son."

Papaji did wait till Namita was twenty-one. She got her BA degree before he embarked on a search for his second son-in-law. She enrolled for a degree in Fine Arts while they waited for a suitable match. Then came this contact from another country, one Tarun Neggill, who lived in a place called Winnipeg in Canada, and who earned a princely salary of 45,000 rupees a month. Suddenly everything moved very fast. There were long distance telephone conversations, followed by a long distance engagement for which the young man's uncle and aunt came as proxy, and the wedding date was fixed. Papaji said Tarun's family had left all arrangements to them; such decent people, he said, they wanted nothing. Just do whatever you can for your *beti*, your daughter, they said, we make no demands.

This time, Bina-Ma was out of her depth; she did not know how to deal with people long distance; she was one of those who still felt uneasy speaking on the telephone. She kept saying she wished their dear little beti did not have to go so far away. But, and she could see it for herself, their little beti was quite an independent young woman now, and she was earning her own living, teaching at a school nearby, and going to the Music and Dance Academy in the evenings. She came home every payday with two saris, in the latest design, for herself and for Bina-Ma; they still did many things together, including music, but Bina-Ma knew things were beyond her now. Canada, so far away. Why did anyone want to go so far away? she asked time and again. She herself had never wanted anything other than this patch of land, this little lake that was dry except in the monsoons, this peacock garden she had grown to love, and all her children and grandchildren close to her.

*****

Namita thought that Bina-Ma, in her deep intuitive way must have known something which she could not articulate, dared not articulate because of her simple belief that if one said out loud anything bad, it would come to pass. She who had so cleverly worked their way out of the tangle of Asha's dowry to everyone's satisfaction, could not do anything for Namita. Because everything bad started much later. After Tarun had left to return to Canada, taking her virginity and her heart with him in a whirlwind of wedding, reception and honeymoon, his parents stayed on, visiting one relative after another. That is when the trouble started, as Namita found out.

A month after Namita's arrival in Winnipeg, Menka took a temporary job at a store run by a friend. The next two weeks were heavenly for Namita. Tarun came home for very long lunchbreaks, and while his parents took their nap, the two of them slipped upstairs and made love on the queen-size bed and talked in whispers. It was then that he told her where the dowry problem had started. He explained that his relatives were to blame, asking his parents what the new daughter-in-law had brought as *dahej* and filling them with dissatisfaction. Then it had mounted up, with her father fuming to a go-between about deceit and hypocrisy. No doubt the go-between had exaggerated everything, Tarun agreed, but his parents' *izzat*, prestige was hurt, badly hurt. And izzat as perceived by others, meant everything , as she should know. They don't want you here, he had said, because they feel insulted that your father did not yield an inch, but don't worry, we just have to wait till they take to you.

Tarun's parents sent between-the-lines messages through go-betweens that they wanted a cash settlement. Of course they did not want dowry. Not at all. They only wanted the traditional gifts, they maintained. Their family's airfare, for example. Five of them had flown at their own expense from Canada at high season fare, and they had assumed, so said the go-betweens, that Papaji would reimburse their fare. And then there was the clothes for family members; they had explicitly said they did not want any because Indian clothes and fashions were unsuited for Canada, but they had implicitly assumed that Papaji would give them cash instead, three suits for the men at five-hundred dollars each. And the wedding itself — what a small affair it had been, certainly not what they had assumed an old, established Jaipur family would provide for them and their guests. But what was past was past. Never mind about the smallness of the wedding, never mind that they had served peanuts instead of almonds and cashews. But they did expect a cash settlement, ten *lakhs* surely was not unreasonable for a foreign-based son-in-law. There were minor confrontations, and then a major one.

******

Two days after Canada Day, Namita saw the morning newspaper on a table and picked it up. She turned to the Business Section. One Indian rupee equals $0.03333, she read. She calculated: 30 rupees equals a dollar, 3,000 rupees equals $100; 100,000 rupees equals $3,333; ten lakh rupees equals $33,330. Two years' salary for Tarun, but fifteen, maybe twenty years salary for her father. A cup of coffee cost a dollar, sometimes more. Thirty rupees for a cup of coffee. Why would anyone ruin a woman's life for a mere year's salary? She could earn that much money easily, not in a year maybe, but in three years; she would work it out with Tarun when he called. Together they could give them what they wanted — $33,000 plus interest — and they could cut themselves free. Together they could do anything they set their mind to in this country. Namita clenched her hand determinedly. Here I shall stay and here my children will be born. I have to be patient. I must not phone him. I must wait.

The next day, Tarun telephoned. The receptionist said she would give Namita a message. She added that he should try again in a few minutes.

Namita was paged, even though she was right there within sight of the receptionist, who knew she was there. Namita had been told that this was the shelter's method: She would be given a message if anyone called, and it was her decision whether or not to call back. If, however, she gave the receptionist a specific request that she should be called to the phone if a specified person called, then she could come to the phone when paged. The shelter advised residents to never to come if paged, but could not forbid them from doing so. She had given Tarun's name and said she wanted to speak with him if he called.

She ran over to the receptionist's desk and was asked to wait. He had been told to call again in a few minutes. "What if he doesn't?" She was frantic.

He called back so she eagerly grabbed the telephone. They spoke in Hindi, as they always did at home.

"How long will you be there?" was his first question. "I have to meet you. Did you get the papers?"

"What papers? The divorce papers? They are a terrible mistake, aren't they? When did you come back? When can you come?"

"Who have you talked to?"

"So many different people; all so sweet; everyone is so helpful ..."

"So who have you talked to? Counsellors? Lawyers?"

"I'm supposed to meet one tomorrow."

"A lawyer?"

"Yes, a Legal Aid lawyer, they said."

"Don't tell them anything till you hear again from me."

"It's all a mistake, isn't it?"

"Yes, it was all a mistake. I'll call back tomorrow. I am calling from work now. I have to run."

Tarun ran to his lawyer's office in the basement of a building which had a restaurant called Best Chinese and Canadian Take-Out, a grocery, and a used-furniture warehouse of sorts. The steps to the basement were littered with styrofoam plates and cups. The smell of soya sauce and French fries assailed one's nose. He knocked on the door and entered. Chalak Singh was in his usual pose — legs on table, cigarette in hand. His turban lay on a sidetable. The basement was hot; a table fan revolved lazily. "Tarun Sahab, come in, come in, what can I do for you?"

"You didn't tell me she would get a lawyer so fast."

"Calm down, Tarun Sahab, here, let me open a cola for you. He got up, went to the refrigerator and took out two cans of pop."

"What are you panicking about? Everything is going according to schedule isn't it? One thing you have to do, my friend, is to get someone to sign an affidavit that you shared an apartment with him from February 4 to June 30. That is, from the day she phoned you from Jaipur to say she was on her way till after she had left your house. If you can find someone, fine, otherwise I can line up a friend who owes me big time, but it should be done well before the hearing, okay? It may not be needed, but it is better to play safe and have proof that the two of you lived at two separate addresses."

Chalak Singh took out his copy of the petition, and scanned it for his notes.

"Another point, my friend, you have to do a little mouth work about what you have claimed. Time to start the ball rolling — tell a few friends about how letdown you feel, that she's cheated on you even before landing here. Make up a story and stick to it. No need for details, but always repeat the same story. Choose the right people — at your workplace, get your immediate supervisor. I don't have to tell you how to go about it: a bit of a preamble apologizing for bringing personal matters to him, and then, with due hesitation about the arranged marriage, the long delay in her arrival, then you let drop about her adultery, never anything specific. Same with your friends at the temple, your workplace, and your classmates in the community college course you are taking. Always the same story."

He checked off a couple of points on another sheet in the folder. "And never forget that the story you tell now must tally with what you've said here — more than a year ago, in March, and you remember the date because it was your birthday, she called you from India and said she was not planning to join you; that takes care of the one-year clause, and mental cruelty number one; imagine how depressed it made you to get that kind of birthday present. But then you took it like a man and wished her well. Next thing you know she calls you from Toronto, last February, when you happened to be visiting your parents — never forget that you moved out to your friend's apartment the day she phoned from Jaipur — and she taunted you that she had made good use of the sponsorship papers and was in Canada but had no plan to join you in Winnipeg — that goes with the mental cruelty claim you've got here," he tapped the petition. "And then, next day she landed on your parent's doorstep, just like that, but you had already moved out."

"But what if I trip on cross examination? You never said she would get a lawyer this fast."

"Calm down, calm down. Here," he pushed a box of tissues and raised the fan speed by a notch. "Cross examination — you are right, you will trip, honest man that you are, my friend, and so here is the solution — NO cross examination. Simple, very simple. Now listen carefully. You have to meet her, talk to her. Remember the main story — your parents are the bad guys. You have to persuade her that if she would play along for a while, and not contest the divorce, you can back get together soon. If she contests it, she will never see you again. Get it? — promise her everything — tell her she must play along and let the divorce go through and all will be well — you'll be in her bed before she turns around; you will live your secret life and love with her and remarry her good and proper as soon as your parents go on their next visit to India. She is not to contest the divorce. That is all she needs to tell her lawyer. She must stand fast on that. No contesting."

Tarun mopped his face. "I have to get back to work." He rushed out.

Chalak Singh placed his feet back on the table and took out a cigarette. "Tarun," he wrote in his appointment book against the date, "one hour consultation, add to Neggill file." His secretary, who came in for only a few hours each week, would take care of making the proper entries on the proper forms and vouchers. He charged his clients half the going rate per hour but always doubled the number of hours he had spent on their behalf.

He opened the second drawer of his desk and poured himself a shot of whiskey. He told himself he should go after some richer cases, maybe get some decent office space, team up with someone else; but all that meant more overhead, more paperwork. Now he netted ninety per cent of whatever he made, especially with cash transactions for small favours. He liked it this way. Taxi drivers, small businessmen who ran small shops in run-down areas of town, most of them from within the community, a few from outside, like Chan-Lee upstairs, who got into trouble time to time from Health Inspectors. Time to warn him about the garbage stink. Another hundred bucks billed for timely advice. Which Lee would not heed, and then there would be more paperwork and more income. No one could blame him, Chalak Singh, of not advising his clients to take preventative measures against possible infringements. But he really should get around to more lucrative deals. If only he could get a pipeline going on marriages of convenience with divorcees, like this Namita once this was over, wouldn't she be happy to sponsor a young man for hard cash? But women were generally too uncooperative. Once they tasted freedom, they held our men in contempt, he thought, and spat out the idea. Women, ugh, it was well he kept his own on short leash.

******

Shayna came with the lawyer that afternoon. He was a tall thin man, balding and weary-looking. "Everything is okay," Namita told him. "My husband phoned this morning and said it was all a mistake."

He patiently explained that the paperwork still had to be done. He advised her to contest the petition, and to ask for spousal support. They were standard procedures that he would go over step-by-step, but first he needed to ask some questions. He opened the file Shayna had given him. It contained a copy of the petition. She tried to snatch it out of the file. How had it gotten there from her bag? Shayna had made a copy of it. Didn't she remember giving her papers to Shayna so they could help her?

She didn't need their help. Her husband had phoned that morning. "Ms Neggill," the lawyer said, "we are here to help you. You are new to Canada, we are not. Please hear me out."

"My husband told me I should not speak to anyone until he called me again."

"Ms Neggill."

"He told me not to speak to anyone."

The lawyer closed his file. "Ms Neggill, you need help. Keep in touch through Shayna."

******

Shayna came the next morning. She had all the papers for income assistance, and she went through each line with Namita, making sure she filled it in correctly. Seeing that Namita was not opening up, she ventured, "The lawyer spoke to me this morning."

"I don't need him. I told you, my husband called me; he is coming soon, maybe this evening."

Shayna spoke softly and slowly, telling her about the difference between emotions and the law. No matter what he said or did now, the legal point was that he had sued for divorce. It would always be her word against his, and he would likely have people to vouch for anything he wanted. Perhaps it would be a good idea, she suggested, for Namita to make some contact with her own ethno-community. The thought had never occurred to her. Now that Shayna had put it into her head, Namita was excited. Of course, she knew where she could go, the temple, the gurudwara, Indian spice stores, restaurants, dozens of places where she could find people from India. Why had it never struck her? But then, where was the need? Tarun had phoned and said it was all a mistake.

He had never taken her to the temple. Every Sunday, her father-in-law went with one of his sons, usually Tarun, for Bhaiyan had no patience to sit cross-legged on the floor for two hours. At dinner, the men spoke about community news and who was getting married when, who was going to India when and for how long. The women soaked up every bit of gossip, and relayed it on the phone to their friends, but it seemed to be the custom of the house that women did not go to the temple.

The next day, Krista came to her at the breakfast table. It had been arranged to transfer Namita to another shelter. Now that the paperwork was underway, Namita could leave Bournedaya House, and enter a Women's Residence run by the Salvation Army. Namita panicked. I can't go, I have to stay, she started crying. Thinking that Namita had gotten attached to the counsellors, Krista described the other shelter. Everything would be the same as here, three meals a day, counsellors to help. It was a much larger place, she would get a bus pass, there would be people to tell her how to get around, she would be fine, absolutely fine, girl, don't you worry. But then Namita told her why she could not leave yet — her husband had said she should not do anything until he called her, and so she had to stay, had to.

Krista gave up. "Okay," she said, "you can stay till he calls, but be careful with him."

"He is not like that," Namita said, thinking to herself, these people would never know how strongly rooted her culture was, how different Tarun was from people here.

Tarun phoned the next morning. He said he would come around that evening. "What is the address?" he asked. Coached by Krista that she should not give the shelter's address to anyone, but could choose Eaton Place as a meeting place, she told him she'd meet him at the bus stop on Carlton, and asked him to name a time. He promised everything would be all right, as long as she stayed where she was and did not speak to anyone.

"He is coming." She ran to Krista. "He said he is coming. Can I go with him?"

"We are a safe house, not a prison," Krista said. "We can't hold you here if you want to go." She felt tired. She knew she was being terse, but she was giving up on this woman. It was no use. You can't help anyone who doesn't want to be helped. If only you could give them a couple of slaps and force them to shape up, she thought. Krista was doubly-tired because Alina had gone back to her husband. If Alina didn't have the good sense to know what she should do after her experience these past two years, why would this young woman? But maybe what she said was true, that his family were pressuring him. What a wimp, she thought, what an anaemic wimp, couldn't stand up to the bullying of a brother and father. But it was her life. Krista felt very tired. It was like bashing your head against a stone wall. If even just one out of ten women would get out of the cycle, even one of every twenty, fifty. If it weren't for the children, she wouldn't be here day after day. Volunteers often left, saying they couldn't take the suffering of the children. Oh god, we insist on licenses for sitting behind the wheel of a car; why don't we have mandatory revocation of parenthood licenses?

Chapter Three

It was the fourth weekend of July. Namita was in the Salvation Army residence. It had been a traumatic experience leaving the all-women facility and coming to this large building and seeing all these people — the faces of the men, many disabled, many with bloodshot hungover eyes, wherever she turned ghoulish sights of men and women who looked, walked, talked differently. She could not figure out who was disabled, who was drunk or drugged, though she was told no one who was drunk would be admitted at night. The women's floor seemed full of young women. Namita felt a chill running up and down her spine when she saw them, their real faces hidden beneath layers and layers of heavy make-up. Every morning everyone was woken up at some unearthly hour and asked to sign that they were in. Donuts and pastries were available in plenty, and there was a lot to eat at every meal, though all she could safely eat was the salad and bread rolls, never knowing what might have been cooked in lard, or what was beef. She ate more donuts than anything else.

Tarun came every day and took her out for a drive. He parked at odd places, and they groped and kissed and made out in a frenzy. He did not speak much, and when he did, it was to say all would be well as long as she let her lawyer allow the divorce to go through without making any demands for herself. He would take care of her; as long as she kept their life a secret from the family, all would be well. He dropped her off at the corner of Henry and Main every day, and she walked back in a daze of pleasure and hope.

She told him of every new step she had taken each day — how her income assistance was in place, how the Housing Authority had given her the go ahead, how her résumé had been typed up by Shayna.... She never questioned him about what he claimed as reasons for filing those papers — how could he have thought for a moment she would have gone with any other man, and what did he mean by mental cruelty? She did not ask him anything. She just lapped up the moments of togetherness and thought of them all night and all day until he came again.

Then he stopped coming. One day, she received papers from the court, sent through Tarun's lawyer. The divorce had been granted. There was no provision for spousal support in the divorce. She had thirty days to appeal. She called Shayna, who called the Legal Aid lawyer. As Namita had instructed him, he had not contested. "But that is not what I meant," she said, "no contesting doesn't mean I want no spousal support."

Another lawyer was assigned to her. He filed for support. Tarun appeared again. He raged and ranted. How dare she appeal and ask for spousal support? He would never come again, never. Because if he did, he just might break every bone in her body. He'd had it. He was through.

In tears, she phoned her new lawyer and told him of how her husband had threatened her. Shayna accompanied her to his office and she signed her complaint. Then all hell broke loose.

Tarun appeared, made her get in the car, drove her out to the highway, stopped the car and raged at her. How dare she lie to her lawyer about him threatening her; he would never come again, never as long as he lived, she was dead to him and he to her. She begged and cried, cried and begged, she'd do anything as long as he promised he would come every day. He made her write to "Dear Lawyer" that she had never complained to him about her husband; there was some serious lapse of communication. Yes, she wanted reconciliation between her husband and herself. But — and this is important — he had never threatened her in any way, why had the lawyer so misunderstood her position? She wrote what he dictated, signed it and gave it to him.

Next day, she called the Legal Aid lawyer and repeated all that she had written. She also said she had met her husband the previous evening and that he had been very angry and said he would never see her again if she did not contact her lawyer, and that she could not live without his daily visit. The lawyer could not figure out what she really wanted.

Shayna met with Krista for a consultation. Krista knew just what was happening — the same seesaw movement that she had seen a thousand times in a hundred different women, but there was nothing concrete they could use. It was his word against hers, and the court had already accepted Tarun's statement that she had been adulterous and cruel.

******

Namita started getting excited at the prospect of having a place of her own. She was getting adept at finding her way around the city on buses, at going to shopping malls and leaving her résumé at every store. She had been at the new shelter for two weeks, and now its familiarity was comforting. She greeted the disabled men by name, joked with the seeming-derelicts who opened the door for her, kept out of the way of the young women on her floor, volunteered around the dining room and lounge.

It was Sunday. Janet, at the reception desk, said there would be a service in the chapel at 10 o'clock, and she'd be glad to take Namita if she felt like it. Namita felt suddenly awake. Why had she not thought of it before? She would go to the temple. Her suitcases had been stored somewhere by the receptionist in the office. She thought she would take a salwar-suit out for the temple. But then she decided her everyday Canadian clothes were good enough. She had washed her clothes the previous evening. One needed clean clothes for the temple, they did not have to be Indian costumes.

She went to Janet and said with some excitement, "I have to find out how to get to 854 Ellice." Janet smiled and said, "Sure, and you know how, right?" Janet knew when to channel people to be independent. She gestured towards the transit information number that was on the bulletin board. "986-5700," Namita said. "You're getting there, Namita," Janet said.

Namita dialled. "Please, how do I get from Main and Henry to 854 Ellice?" she asked, while Janet nodded approval.

"Take 18 going south to Garry and Graham, and then 14 going west on Ellice. Do you know the cross street?"

"No, but you've been helpful. Thank you."

Every phone conversation boosted her self-confidence. "Please" at the beginning of every conversation, "Thank you" at the end. The rule was so simple. If she could just work on her accent. She seemed to stress the wrong part of words; she knew she was doing it wrong, but couldn't figure out what was right for each different word. Even simple words like adult. Who would have thought it was "A-dult" with a long wide *Ah* instead of the stress being on the *dul* as she had thought all these years? She watched television all day, trying to watch the women's mouths as they spoke. When she told that to Janet one day, Janet nodded approvingly, and suggested she watch the news channel if she really wanted to learn the accent. But, of course, the lounge TV was usually on a sports channel.

Namita had another wash, and checked that the bus pass was in her handbag. She carried her handbag close to her at all times, not trusting the safety of the locker in her room. Then she came down, and said good-bye to Janet. "Have a good day," Tim hobbled ahead of her to open the door.

"Thank you, Tim," and he gave her a high five. On the first day he did it, she had instinctively shrunk away from his wasted hand, associating it with leprosy, that highly-infectious disease so visible everywhere in India. Even now, she was not wholly at ease with Down's Syndrome and Thalidomide victims, of whom there were two in the lounge on most days, but now she saw them as people, with names and faces. Tim, Jon, Barry, Brandon. Rehab, stabilization unit, detox, drunk tank. Her vocabulary grew every day, and her self-confidence.

"You've come a long way, baby," was counsellor Dorothy's

favourite phrase, even though she was quick to point out all kinds of sexism in television commercials that Namita could never have seen on her own in a hundred years. Namita repeated it to herself many times each day.

The bus on route 18 took its time coming. But she did not mind. By now, she took bus rides in stride, asking the driver for any direction she needed. Always start the sentence with "Excuse me."

"Excuse me, could you please tell me where I get off for Garry and Graham?"

"That's Winnipeg Square you're looking for, ma'am?"

"I need to transfer to 14."

"Yep, Winnipeg Square it is. Sure will."

It was a bright sunny day, not a cloud in the sky. Oh the world was so beautiful. 14 took an even longer time coming. Sundays, Janet had said, Sundays are real slow.

"Excuse me, could you please tell me where I get off for 854 Ellice?"

"Should be past Arlington, I'd guess."

"It is the Hindu temple."

"Okay, right, no problem."

Namita always stood behind the driver, even if the bus was empty. In the last day or two, she had felt safe enough to sit on the seat behind him, if there was a seat.

"Your stop next."

"Thank you. Have a good day." she said.

"You take care," he said.

The temple. Her heart raced. She was entering the temple. She bowed; she touched the steps with her fingers and raised her fingers to her forehead. The sound of sacred music floated to her ears as someone opened the double doors and entered ahead of her. She could see two women taking off their coats and she followed them. She took off her shoes, went into the washroom, washed her hands, and followed the women into the prayer hall, which was half full, it being past eleven o'clock. Holy holy holy space.

She was transported into it; the altars were a kaleidoscope of lights and tinsel streamers; she closed her eyes and let the music sink into her being. She took her seat at the side, almost at the foot of the altar of the Divine Mother. The Mother was seated on her tiger in a resplendent halo of multicoloured minilights that revolved first in one direction, then in another; the gold circles on her red sari glimmered, her bare sword was raised, the large diamond on her crown flashed. Glory glory glory Durga Mata, Divine Mother Supreme. Namita closed her eyes and knew she was home at last. Glory glory glory.

People kept coming, in ones and twos. Namita closed her eyes, and let the music sink in. Soon, her thinking process came alive again, and she recognized that some of the singers were rather off-key. She rebuked herself. Too much knowledge of music, that was her problem. She would not think, only feel. She closed her eyes.

"Before we have prasad distribution, we have announcements. It is our custom to give a special welcome to first time visitors. Please identify yourselves so we can greet you." The woman next to Namita, nudged her, but Namita only smiled. "Next time," she whispered, "maybe next time."

"You are invited to join the preeti bhoj downstairs...." Everyone rose and the line to the basement started forming.

"That is the best part, good food," said the older woman next to her, winking. "You are new, I see. What is your name?"

"Namita."

"Speak Hindi?"

"Yes, I'm from Jaipur."

The other woman immediately switched to Hindi. She wanted to know Namita's full name, which Namita evaded; whether she was married or single, married; whether she had children, no, not yet; whether she worked in an office, she was still looking for a job; where did she live? north of downtown; so how long had she been here? six months; what did her husband do?

He's abandoned me. That would have been a proper reply, but Namita knew it was time to run; she said, "Excuse me," and stepped out of the line. The young woman who had spoken to her earlier, and had watched her as she was being interrogated, motioned to her to join in front of her.

"My turn to grill, though I don't speak Hindi since I am from Kerala," she said with a laugh. "My name is Charu," she said, "what is yours?"

"Namita."

"New to Winnipeg?"

"Yes, have you been here long?"

"Six years."

"Like it?"

"Yes. As nice a place as any. You?"

"Yeah. I've never seen a friendlier place. Please, thank you, have a good day, take care, keep well. People have been so overwhelming in their kindness."

"Really? Are we talking about the same place?"

"Don't you think so?"

"Dunno. Like, do they really mean it? Or is it just a lip-service thing?"

"Really. People have been so wonderful."

Charu shrugged. "Guess you've been lucky."

"Come every Sunday?" Namita asked.

"Whenever I can. By yourself?"

"Yeah."

"Me too. And glad to be." She said that with a finality that could not be missed.

Namita looked at her, and suddenly felt herself smiling.

"You too, huh?" she said, probing cautiously.

"You too, no!!!" surprised and pleased. "I thought so when you slipped out of that interrogation in a hurry, but wasn't sure. You don't have to answer everyone's questions, you know."

"But how does one escape? I guess I have to learn how to dodge the questions without turning people off."

"You'll learn."

"Lovely altars."

"Too glitzy for my taste, but I guess it's okay."

"He never brought me here," Namita said.

"Mine neither, not after the first year anyway. Pigs."

Both smiled even more broadly at each other.

"This is just so good. Imagine running into you, that the very first person I run into should be you." Namita said.

Charu stepped out of the line and drew her off too. They moved back into the centre of the hall "We can talk now. Downstairs it is too messy. So where did you find your helpful people?"

Namita did not want to open up that widely yet. She did not answer.

Charu nodded. "It's okay. Time enough." She led the way to rejoin the line. "Just that I sure didn't find any here, and I wanted to know where you had. See them? All these ladies, not one has any real empathy. Men are like that, they said. They'll come around, they said. Don't wash dirty linen in public, that's their favourite line. Which makes me wonder how many of them are putting up with horse manure and not letting on."

"Not one will help?"

"Not that I know of."

"I came here thinking I'd get some help from someone who'd understand our culture.

"Wrong place. But there are some out there, don't let me crush your optimism. Some of our women are in every area: social work, employment counselling, ESL, university; good work they do too, but they don't often come to temples. There is Madhu Aunty who works for Psychiatric Services, Prem Aunty who works for Family Services, and Maru who's been in all kinds of women's organizations. I could give you a whole list of names if you wish, and of some of the helpful ones who go to the gurudwara. But these women who really care come here only once in a long while. This place is for those who love gossip and good food."

"You are cynical."

"And why shouldn't I be? Like, when he raped me three times one night when I was four months pregnant, and I miscarried, know what one of these prissy ladies said, Don't mind it, you'll conceive again. You pour out your heart to them, but do they see or feel anything?"

"We shouldn't be talking such things here."

"God doesn't mind. He knows it already, remember."

They stopped whispering as the line wound down the basement stairs. The food was indeed good. And for Namita, after four weeks of donuts, it was manna from heaven.

They clasped hands before taking leave of each other. It had been wonderful, but it did not yet feel right to exchange phone numbers or to say one didn't have a phone.

******

"Downtown," Namita said, as her first choice when filling out the housing form. She got a wide choice of addresses. Downtown is the easiest, Shayna said, slum landlords a-plenty. Shayna helped her sort through an accommodation list and came up with four possible addresses. She was sorry she couldn't come with Namita, but she gave her some necessary pointers and promised she'd advise her once Namita narrowed the four choices to two.

Namita chose the two that were closest to bus routes.One was a small house on the corner of Sargent and a small sidestreet, where the owner wanted to rent out one of two rooms on the top floor; the other was in a three-storey apartment block with four suites on each floor, two houses from Isabel and three blocks from Portage. The vacant unit was on the second floor; it was an efficiency suite with a kitchenette, a built-in dining nook and a very large walk-in closet. Shayna pointed out the plus/minus of both places. The homeowner seemed friendly and said tenants could use the laundry downstairs and her phone as long as it was for local calls; but she was old, the stairs creaked, and there was only one front door. The apartment was crummy-looking, it had windows on two sides of the building but overlooked a garbage bin, tenants had to take their laundry out to a laundromat, and had to arrange and pay for telephone service, but the caretaker was a strong young man who lived in the building and he seemed a helpful guy.

They decided on the apartment.

Sandy Ketts was a volunteer at the shelter. He was a full-time student at the University of Winnipeg, in his graduating year, but even so, he came three afternoons a week to the shelter, just as he had for the last three years. He was a strapping Adonis of a young man, "tall and black, with a set of teeth one could die for", as Namita heard one of the younger women say to another. Whenever Namita heard a word or phrase that interested her, she jotted it down in a little engagement calendar that a cousin had given her before she left Jaipur. She had written only two entries in it. On February 6th, she had entered: "Left Jaipur for Delhi with Papaji and Bina-Ma. On February 10th she had written: "Writing this in the boarding lounge of Indira Gandhi International Airport. Left Chachiji's flat at midnight by taxi with Papaji and Bina-Ma. Checked in at 1:30 am. Another two hours to go. Can't believe I am really leaving."

Since coming to this shelter, she had written something every day. She wrote in tiny letters about people she had talked to that day; often she wrote phrases she had heard and liked. "Teeth one could die for" had an interesting ring to it. Tarun has hair one could die for, she practised saying; indeed he did, a shock of thick, black hair that one could run one's fingers through. "Eat crow" she had heard someone say to someone else at breakfast. It took her a long while to figure out the words, let alone the meaning of that phrase, and then only when Janet had told her.

Sandy was the most wonderful guy she had seen among all the wonderful people she had the good fortune to meet during the past four weeks. She had a whole list of his repartees. He was so handsome, the middle-aged women in the shelter would ask him, "How can such a good-looker be so patient too?" or something similiar. He had a different answer each time.

"Lot of hard work, ma'am, I do nothing but practise patience from midnight to 3 am every night."

"Not easy, ma'am, takes me thirty minutes, four times a day, to floss my teeth."

"Take it from me, ma'am, it is hard work being so handsome."

He always addressed all women as "ma'am," just as Krista said, "girl." Janet made a point of calling everyone by their first name, but Krista had explained that people's need for anonymity had something to do with her habit.

Namita wrote down these thoughts and trivia in the minutest possible letters in the January and February sections of her book;

and now she was into March. She wrote what someone else said of Sandy the previous evening: "one gorgeous hunk of flesh."

She repeated the words to him this morning. "I am learning," she said, "two phrases every day, and I'll soon be Canadian, eh?"

He smiled. "Sally Hemmings," he said. "Add that for today. What happens when the beauty of Africa gets mixed with the skin colour of Europe."

"Your mother?" she asked.

"I guess there's no reason you should know her," he said. "She was President Jefferson's slave lady-love."

She told Sandy of her decision to take the apartment instead of the room in the house. "I'll be out of your hair in another week," she said. "Out of your hair" was another phrase that fascinated her. Some of the young women on her floor had such wild hair, she could imagine little birds swarming in and out of their hairdos.

"We'll miss you, but I'm glad for you. You're really getting there, Namita. You can be proud of yourself."

"You've come a long way, baby," she said, repeating Dorothy's phrase because it sounded so good.

"Yes, ma'am, you've come a long way."

Sandy wanted to know more about the move. Did she have any furniture? No. Well, he could help get some from Goodwill or Value Village. Did she need a phone connection? Not yet. Don't wait too long, a phone is one's lifeline, you know. What about pots and pans? He could salvage some easily enough. And a bed, don't forget to sleep and breathe. He'd find out about getting a bed. He made note of all this. He phoned the caretaker and said it would be good if she could move on Sunday instead of Monday, because he wasn't free to help on Monday.

Tarun phoned on Thursday. He had been away, he said. Slowly he got her talking, and soon she told him everything, including where she was moving and when.

She was impatient for Sunday to come around again. She was at the temple by ten o'clock. There were hardly a handful of people. She helped them spread bedsheets on the carpets. Tarun came in, saw her, and quickly went downstairs. She went into the foyer. Among the men's coats, she recognized his, and put her face into it; a whiff of Player's No. 5 suffused her face. She looked among the footwear, and recognized his shoes. She bent and touched them with her fingers and raised her fingers to her forehead. Her first action had been deliberate, but her second had been reflexive. She had gone looking for his coat, but the shoes had caught her eyes unawares. She had touched his shoes, she told herself. What was she doing? And yet, and yet, it had come so naturally ... She was about to enter the prayer hall again when she noticed that Tarun was already there, standing in front of Siva's altar on the men's side of the hall. She quickly walked backward and out, then took the stairway to the basement.

Charu was standing by herself near the library door. Namita joined her. One of the women in the kitchen came out and addressed Charu in saccharine tones, "Charu, we have enough volunteers today; I think you can go upstairs." With equally cloying sweetness, Charu said, "Oh, aunty, do let us roll the chappatis so you can listen to the bhajans upstairs in peace." The woman turned away disapprovingly. Namita and Charu giggled discreetly. Charu said, "Some of them think the likes of us will pollute the food that is made for the offering. " Another woman, on her way to the kitchen, smiled at them and said to Charu, "Could you please check if there are enough paper napkins for both prasad and lunch. If not, you know whom to ask for the key."

"Nice lady," Namita said.

"Yes, she's a nice person."

"Glad to hear that. You scared me the other day about the people here."

"Okay, maybe I was thinking only of the nasty ones. Tell me again," Charu said, "did you really find white people helpful like you said last week?"

"Yes, don't you?"

"I am not sure. They are probably well-meaning but they are so ignorant, like they have no clue of the world out there, no clue at all. They have such stupid ideas about India, the people I work with anyway, like they assume I am in this deep hole because of arranged marriages. And so I have to tell them about it, that it is not an oppressive thing at all, that ninety per cent of Indo-Canadians they see here were married that way and that most of them are probably happier than most couples here. That parents knew what they were looking for — someone from a decent family, with the same background, language, food habits — stuff like that helps people get along. You may never know a guy until too late, and that is the simple truth whether you have an arranged marriage or not. I mean, there is this woman who works with me who lived with a guy for years, got married to him last year, and now they are getting divorced."

"I've never tried telling anyone anything. Maybe that is why I find them so nice. How can they understand anything about life in another country so far away? Mine was an arranged marriage, and as you say, most of them seem to work out all right."

"Awful thing is, mine wasn't quite one. I said no to the first two guys my parents had me meet, and then said yes to this jerk, even though he sure wasn't their choice once they met him. My Dad, especially, kept saying I was being carried away by looks. And I guess Dad was right. This guy had a kind of sex appeal, like, and I insisted."

Namita thought of Tarun, sitting upstairs. "Does your husband come here?" she asked.

"When we first came to Canada, we'd come together. But then when things started going wrong, he would come once in a while and I once in a while but never on the same day. Then when word got around that he was beating me up, he stopped coming and of course he didn't want me coming either. We just dropped out of everything, temple, community parties, everything. It is an izzat thing, as you know. When a man has wronged a woman, whether his conscience ever troubles him or not, his status among his friends is affected by her very presence, and all he wants is for her to disappear from his social circle. But I didn't. So he left for Vancouver, and I got the house. A good enough deal, don't you think?"

A woman came to them, greeted Charu and turned to Namita. "You are a new face?"

"I am Namita."

"Namita what?"

"Give me some job to do, please."

The woman shrugged, smiled, and went her way.

Namita whispered, "Oh, I do so feel tempted to say I am Tarun's wife."

Charu raised her eyebrows. "Tarun? Wow. Be sure I am here when you spring that one on them. I'd love to see their face."

"He comes often?"

"But of course, and ladies with daughters have been after him ever since he came to Winnipeg five years ago."

"I've been married more than two years."

"Really! I wonder how many people know that?"

"Are you in the know of things? Like what people know and are talking about?"

"No one talks anything personal to me, directly, as you can see, but gossip can be retrieved in many ways. Let's have some fun."

Charu went closer to the kitchen, and said loudly to no one in particular, "I hear Menka Neggill is expecting."

"High time, too. The way young women keep putting off starting their families, pah," said one.

"So what is the latest about Tarun Neggill?" said another. "Such a nice young man and to have such a terrible thing happening. Such bad luck. Poor boy."

"What? What? Tell me, I haven't heard."

"Oh, it is all over the community. Poor boy, his wife was cheating on him all the time, and he is caught in a messy divorce."

"Really? I didn't even know he was married. Even the other day, at Pran's wedding, I was teasing him — he was next in line — and he didn't tell me he was married."

Namita felt nauseated. She left Charu and slipped upstairs. She stayed long enough to accept the sacred flame and fruits, and then hurried out. Charu, who had joined her, pressed her hand. "Stay a bit. Let's go out together. It is not true what I said about Menka. I am sorry I started on anything." Namita returned the pressure but then rushed away.

"How could he? How could he spread such lies?"

*****

Sandy was there at four o'clock as he had said. Janet was not on duty, but the usual crowd of men were there. They were so happy for her. Jon helped with the suitcases. Tim high-fived her all the way to the car. Sandy drove her out to their bye-byes. Lovely people, Namita said, such lovely people.

"This is where I study," Sandy said, driving around the university block. "Nice place. You should think of taking courses here some time, maybe, and upgrade yourself." He looped back to Isabel and located her new home.

"I have put the bed in already," he said. "Buddy of mine has a van so I figured I'd do it when he could help."

The bed, pots and pans, a chair and a table — all were in place already. Sandy carried the suitcases upstairs, Namita apologizing for their weight, and he shrugging away her thanks. He went back to the car, and brought in two bags of groceries. Namita expressed her surprise. After leaving the temple, she had not been thinking of anything at all. She had spent the afternoon crying.

Sandy put the milk and butter in the refrigerator, the cereal boxes, tea, instant coffee, sugar and bread in the cabinet. "That's all I could think of," he said, "There is a 7-Eleven convenience store just down the road, if you need more milk, you have some money, right?"

He kept up a flow of conversation, "Be sure to run the water a few minutes every morning before drinking it, some of these old places.... Gee, we need to get a shower curtain for you.... Look, you can even see Isabel from here, and the bus stop is just around the corner ... I have got two blankets.... Look, here is the thermostat if you need to raise the heat..."

"Oh, Sandy," she kept saying, "Oh, Sandy, you are so kind I could cry."

"Oh, no, ma'am, you can't because I didn't remember to buy tissues."

He gave the apartment a onceover, then led her out. He locked the door and gave her the key. "Tomorrow is your 'official opening'. Wish I could be here to celebrate, but think of me. Now I have to rush off after dropping you at the shelter," he said.

"I forgot to tell Tim I am coming back for the night," Namita said, "He is going to be puzzled when he sees me."

"Remember, ma'am, I am always only a shout away. Leave me a message any time you need any kind of help, any time of day, Don't hesitate. Janet has my number but here is my card — made it on the computer, isn't it neat?"

******

Namita opened the door to her apartment. Gone was the excitement of the previous evening. It was bare, the plaster peeling from the bathroom ceiling, the glass panes grimy with dust and cooking oil, the floor covered with a pathetic patchy carpet with cigarette burns.

She clutched the key in her hand, and went out for a walk. It was a warm day. Every house had children and adults wearing little clothing, splashing in wading pools, sitting under colourful umbrellas, pop cans in hand. The houses looked trim and painted on the outside, but were probably as rundown inside as hers. Or maybe not. "There is a difference between owner-lived houses and rentals," Shayna had said, "a huge difference." She felt better after an hour of walking, and went back. "Home," she said to herself, "A place of my own."

She bolted the door behind her, opened wide the window in the kitchen, and lay down. She must have slept, for the knock on the door jolted her. She quickly sloshed her face, washed her mouth, and waited for Sandy's voice. Sandy, good Sandy, she thought. What was he bringing her now? The knock was repeated. It is me, he said. She gasped in excitement. Tarun. She opened the door. He came in, looked around, sat on the only chair in the room. He did not bother to take off his shoes for clearly the carpet did not warrant it.

"Nice location, very convenient," he said. "Less than half a block from the bus route."

She did not say anything. He came to her, and led her to the bed. Despite herself, her body subconsciously responded. He could sense it. "I miss you," he said. "You looked so sweet yesterday, I wanted to hug you right then and there, but you disappeared so fast."

Again her body responded despite her uncertainty. His feet worked their way out of his shoes. And she had no control over her body.

"Can I come again?" he asked. "Please, can I come again? I miss you so much."

"Any time you want," she heard herself saying. "Any time."

He came every evening that week and the next week. Even though she had acute cramps at night, she received him and received him as though she were an ocean of waiting. During the mornings, she brooded and cried, wondering where all this was leading to, but come afternoon she waited in a frenzy of desire. When the milk carton emptied, she bought a new one, and some fruit. She did not use the stove or cook anything. She was an ocean of desire, an ocean of waiting. She did not go to the temple that Sunday, for her temple promised to come to her every day. One evening, late in the week, as they lay spent, she started thinking of all the things she meant to talk about every morning which she forgot all about every evening. She looked at her bare arms lying around his head of hair and marvelled at how she had filled out in the last few weeks. "All those donuts have made me fill out, don't you think?" she said. "Soon I might even become as filled out as Menka, and you would like that, wouldn't you?"

He rose. He propped her against the headboard with one hand and swung his other hand across her face. Back and forth. Back and forth. He punched her on her stomach. Then he left. Namita knew now, beyond a doubt, that what she had hoped was merely her exaggerated fear and imagination about Manka and Tarun was true.

He did not come again. She went to the temple on Friday evening and sat quietly for two hours until closing time. Then she went home and lay on her back. She went to the temple on Saturday afternoon, and sat quietly while the Tamil group had their prayer meeting in a language she could not understand. She went home and lay on her back. She went to the temple on Sunday morning and sat quietly near Durga Mata's altar long before anyone else came. She did not know what went through her mind. She was an ocean, but not waiting for anything. Water lapped against stones, wind sighed across waves.

He came again on Monday. She opened the door on hearing his voice because he was her husband, though her lawyer called him her "ex-husband." Tarun forced himself on her. Then he slapped her. "I don't want you coming to the temple," he said. "Don't you dare come to the temple. Unless you want to get yourself killed one of these days." He deliberately took the duplicate key she had been given, that he knew was near the sugar bottle in the kitchen cabinet, and added it to his keychain. Then he left.

She pulled a chair close to a window, pulled a blanket around herself and sat, looking out. There was a narrow gap between her apartment building and the next one, through which she could see the main road. She sat looking at the cars as they flitted through the gap. She slept for a while on the bed before taking up her vigil again at the window. Next morning, she sat there again, and started counting cars, timing them on her watch. Each time, she waited till the second hand came to 12 before she started her count. There were 16 cars one minute, 14 another minute, 12 the next, only 10 once. She jotted down the numbers on the white border of the *Lance* newspaper that was left outside the door once a week. All night she heard someone pacing outside her room; there were occasional scratches on her door. She cowered in her bed and fell asleep early morning. Next day, there were 22 cars many of the times she was counting. Wednesday mornings the traffic is busy, she noted. She had been nibbling at a loaf of bread in the refrigerator and sipping milk from the carton. Both were finished by Wednesday morning. She did not eat anything after that. She sipped from a glass of water. When she used the toilet, she did so with her eyes on the window. She did not shower. She did not want to be caught naked. She lay cowering in bed all night. Someone turned the lock but no one came in. There were footsteps outside her door all night. Someone scratched on the door several times. In the early morning, she fell asleep for a few hours. She rose, brushed her teeth and opened the refrigerator. It was empty except for a wilted cauliflower. She filled her glass with water and placed it on the floor next to her bed. For the next 24 hours she lay in bed, tucking herself smaller and smaller under the blanket.

Someone turned the lock but no one came in. Again there were footsteps outside her door all night. Someone scratched on the door several times.

As soon as it was morning, she put on her coat over her nightshirt, clutched two quarters in one hand, Sandy's card in the other, rushed down to the 7-Eleven and dialled his number. His answering machine came on. "Sandy, Sandy," she sobbed, "please help, I need help, Sandy, please." She rushed back, expecting to have locked herself out, but strangely the door was open. She looked into the bathroom and the closets to make sure there was no one else in the apartment, bolted the door, and cowered in bed all day.

There was a knock around five o'clock. "Namita, ma'am, it's me, Sandy," She knew someone was at the door but could not hear the words. "Sandy Ketts, I picked up your call only now. I'm so sorry, but I had to go to Carberry last night, and came back just now. I am so sorry I never thought to check my answering machine."

She wanted to go to the door, but it was so far away.

"Ma'am, Ms Neggill, it's me, Sandy. You called me this morning," he repeated his phone number, "Are you okay?"

After a moment, he spoke again, "Namita, ma'am, I'm going to get the caretaker to open the door. Don't worry. It's Sandy."

She rose, unlocked the chain bolt and door, and fell against him. "Take me home," she said. He held her shivering body close to himself. "There, there," he said, stroking her as one would a wet squirrel. "There, there. Everything's okay. You're safe."

He gathered a few of her needs, toothbrush, comb, some clothes, and threw them into a 7-Eleven bag that lay on the top of the kitchen counter. He wrapped her in the blanket and led her down to his car. On his cell phone he called the shelter. "I am bringing Namita in. We need a room for her."

Chapter Four

"You can stay as long as you need to, Namita," Janet said. "It's too soon to be on your own."

"I have to leave sometime, Janet."

"Take it a step at a time. Come back for the nights."

Namita took her advice. During the day, she lived in her apartment; she bought some groceries; she even ventured as far as Dino's and bought spices, wheat flour, lentils and a skillet. She cooked and ate her lunches; she washed up. She took bus trips until suppertime and then returned to the shelter. On Friday afternoon she felt she was ready. "You need all the beds you can get on the weekends," she joked to Janet and Sandy.

Saturday morning Tarun was at the door. She was in the kitchen, putting a saucepan of water on the stove. They talked through the locked door in Hindi. He apologized for his behaviour. He had been frantic, he said, at not finding her there all these nights. Please, he begged, please let us talk. He did not know what devil had got into him; he must have been mad, he must have been out of his mind, to say and do what he had done. Please.

She let him in. He did look distraught, and she could feel her body responding, and he sensed it was so. He was cautious. There were now been two chairs at the table. Shayna having given her a folding chair before she left the shelter. He sat on one, she sat on the other, the table between them.

"We can work things out," he said. "They, my parents, are going to India this winter." He went on with family news — several weddings back home, they would be away for six months — he and Namita could work things out, if she would only be patient and accept his apologies. He berated himself again, expressed how devastated he was. Her mother had phoned again, he said.

"Again?"

She had phoned last month and Bhaiyan had said they were both away for the evening.

"Indeed."

And she had phoned two nights ago, about midnight, and Tarun had answered.

"And what was your explanation for me not being at home at midnight? Did you tell her I was away in my lover's arms?"

Tarun's hand rose threateningly but he controlled himself. "You know it was a necessary lie," he said. "I explained that right at the beginning."

"Of course," she said.

"I told her you would call her back." He looked around. "You still have no phone?"

"I don't have that kind of money. If I had got some spousal support, maybe..." she was amazed at her own audacity in goading him.

His face got all puffed up. He is rather ugly, she thought, with surprise.

He changed the topic. "You've set up the place well," he said.

"I am boiling some tea. Maybe you'd like some?"

She rose and went to the kitchenette. He took it as an invitation. He followed her and stretched his hand to her shoulder, slowly stroking it as he drew her closer. She lifted the saucepan and flung the boiling tea on his arm and side; he staggered, and leaned his hand against the counter. She brought the empty saucepan bottom down on his hand.

"Get out of my house," she said. "And don't you dare come back."

From the kitchen corner she took a dirty broomstick that had probably been there through six tenants, and shoved it against him, propelling him out the door. She fastened the chain bolt. She switched on the light and went to the kitchen to brew some fresh tea.

Then she left the tea untasted and cried, knowing all those deliberate actions were just that, actions deliberately gone through. "You have a long way to go, baby," she told herself, knowing she would gladly give all she had gained for a night in his arms.

The next morning, she rose early, had a shower, took a $20 bill from her handbag, and went down to the 7-Eleven. She bought a tube of toothpaste and asked for all the change in quarters. She went to the phone booth and dialled her mother. When she heard Bina-Ma's voice, she thought she might cry, but she did not. Indeed, her voice came out light and happy, "Bina-Ma, how wonderful to hear your voice. How are you? How are Akhil, Nikhil, Papaji?" Bina said, "Beti, it is so comforting to hear your voice, we've been so worried, haven't heard from you in weeks, no letters, no phone calls. We've been so worried. Are you well?"

"Of course I am okay. I promise I'll write you a long letter soon, but now you give me the news. Tell me everything." It suddenly occurred to her that they might have written letters to her that had never reached her. She added, "Everything, even if you've written about it already."

Bina-Ma talked about each person at home and around them. "Before I forget," she said, "Did you get your Krishna intact?"

"What Krishna?"

Then her mother explained. Seth Govind Sahab had come by some two-three months ago, and had noticed Namita's wooden Krishna standing on the bookshelf and had wanted to know why she had not taken it with her as she had promised she would. Bina-Ma had made excuses about her over-stuffed suitcases, and he had said he would send it to her by airmail properly packaged, and had taken down Namita's Winnipeg address. Ever since, he had been asking her father whether they had heard from her about its safe arrival. "It should have reached you by now," Bina-Ma said anxiously.

"It will, Ma, it will. I'll let you know the minute I lay my hands on it."

"It will bring you luck, beti, it is your own special Kanhaiya, your own special charm against the world. Carved with your name on it, that is what Seth Govind Sahab said. You know his line."

"Yes, Ma, *dane dane par likha hai khanewale ka naam....*" (on every grain is written the name of the person for whom it was sown; millions the takers, but the Giver is ever the same, Ram).

"But tell me, sweetheart, are you all right?"

"I went through some tough times, Ma, but I'm fine now."

"I could feel it, sweetheart, I could feel it. But once your Kanhaiya comes home, you will be fine."

"I have to go, now Ma. I love you all; I love you Ma. Take care."

Namita leaned against the booth and closed her eyes. Bina-Ma knew, had known all along, would always know and feel. Across the world she felt her mother's arms around her and she pressed her face into the sweet smell of her milk-wet bodice where lay the ocean of nectar, now and forever hers to sip.

She needed to clear her head of all the chaos that assailed her. She walked towards Portage. The morning traffic was building up. She walked quickly and reached the relatively quieter side of Memorial Boulevard. The fountains were flowing. The grass was wet from the automatic sprinklers that came on in the early morning. She kept to the paved paths. "Come on, come on," she told herself, "Quieten yourself so you can hear what Kanhaiya has to say."

As a child, her secret trysts were in the peacock garden with Krishna-Kanhaiya. She talked to him incessantly, tugged at all his many statues, of stone, of ceramic, of red clay, tweaked his stone ears, threatened to take away his flute, to break all the peacock feathers that she had picked up and tied with strings to his crown, unless he came pronto and talked to her and told her what to do about her homework, about mother's illness, about the lice on her head that she had picked up at school, about every problem she had. And he had always told her. Never in so many words, but in his own mischievous way he talked to her whenever she asked him anything. The peacock garden. She knew why she had not written or phoned her mother or anyone else back home. But why had she never gone to the peacock garden in all these days? And what insanity had made her leave her Kanhaiya just so she could cram her suitcases with saris and trinkets? But she had now come to her senses. She felt herself growing lighthearted. "Okay, Kanhaiya, let us think this through. How do I get you home?"

She heard drumbeats. Not the beats of the *tabla* to which she had danced at the Academy of Music and Dance. But they transported her just the same. In one of her Fine Arts theory courses, she had learned about dances from all over the country, little snippets so they could study the common elements and compare the differences between various dance styles. The Bharata Natyam dance they studied was a Nataraja dance, and the song was in Tamil, about how the god of dance kept his promise to the sages and came in person to dance at the temple of Thillai. Their dancemaster had insisted they should know the meaning of the words they danced to, no matter what the language it was in. He had given them a lecture on Siva iconography and made them repeat his own mantra — "Blessed is he who realizes that Thillai the eternal city is located in the heart of man."

The drumbeats were coming from a tepee set up in front of the Legislative Building, a protest sit-in being staged by native people. She remembered that she had seen it on the television news while at the shelter.

"Okay, Kanhaiya, I think I get it, I have been a bit of a clod about our garden, thinking it was beyond me, but I won't now on. Next, what do we do?"

She could phone Menka and ask directly, but there was always the likelihood that Menka would lie through her teeth. She could write to her mother-in-law, but even if the poor woman wanted to be on her side, she was under her husband's thumb and would never be allowed to write her, or speak on the phone.

She should have asked Tarun if there were any letters for her, but now it was too late for that. It had felt good to "beat the shit out of him" — she savoured the phrase she had picked up at the shelter from one of the young women — but that was over and done with. No regrets. It was for the best. There was no other option. She had to go in person and retrieve her Krishna.

She went back to her apartment. As she reached her door, her neighbour's opened, and a young woman stepped out, carrying a toddler. "Hi," she said, "I'm Jane, this is Tyler, and this is King." She put down the blue-eyed child, and locked the door. The little dog frisked around and scratched on the wall. The toddler ran up and down twice before she could double check that she had locked the door. "Just knock if you need any help," she said. "I'm always home. I have a daughter who goes to school. So I spend much of the day walking her to and back from school, morning, lunch-hour and afternoon. But otherwise I'm home during the day. Except when we figure we'll spend an hour in the playground before heading for school. Right, Tyler? Nice day, isn't it?"

Namita said, "Have a good day."

"You too."

Namita had a shower and took out a clean set of clothes. She combed her hair back and tied it in a neat ponytail. She looked around the apartment for a bag to hold her Kanhaiya when she retrieved him from her in-laws' house, but couldn't find any. Her eyes alighted on a plastic baseball bat that Sandy had found in one of the closets. He had not thrown it out with the newspapers that the previous tenant had stacked up in the same closet. Sandy had propped it up against the wall near her bed. It was made of black plastic, but appeared as though it was a real bat. "You never know when it might come handy," he had joked. "A quick and decisive wallop can be very effective, even with a light weapon." Too bad she hadn't spotted the bat yesterday, she thought, it would have made it even easier to repel Tarun. That had felt so good. She would take the bat now.

She already knew the bus routes for where she wanted to go. Bus pass and two loonies in her pocket, bat in hand, she set out. She overshot her bus stops on both the first bus and the connector, so had to wait and retrack each time. No matter, she had all afternoon to get where she wanted to go. She thought of Krista and her ode of praise to the transit system and how great it was to have a bus pass.

As she walked towards the in-laws' familiar and hated house, she felt a shiver of fear and anticipation. "Kanhaiya," she said, "my Kanhaiya, be with me now and always." She went up the steps and rang the bell. She hoped Menka would open the door and not her father-in-law. No such luck. But maybe it was lucky, because Menka would have peeped through the peephole and told the others who it was and perhaps they would have refused to open the door. But of course, the macho pit bull didn't bother to use the peephole. He was in his usual house clothes — striped pyjamas and sleeveless sweater. He opened the door, and belligerently said, "What are you doing here?" She slipped under his elbow to enter the house. "How dare you," he said and grabbed her by her parka. She wielded her bat to keep him off her, then walked in. She looked around the living room. Kanhaiya was not there. Where else would he be but in Menka's room? She ran up the stairs, right into Menka who had come out of her room and was standing at the door with popped eyes. Downstairs, her mother-in-law had come out of her room and was trying to hold back her husband from chasing Namita up the stairs. Namita elbowed Menka out of her way, walked into Menka's room and sure enough, her Krishna was there, on the stereo stand. She swept him to herself, and started to walk down.

"How dare you," her father-in-law was saying, having pushed his wife away, "Put that down at once."

"Just try stopping me," she said. He lunged at her as he climbed step-by-step. She backed up on to the upper landing, saw the canister vacuum cleaner sitting behind her, and pushed it down the stairs. The moment she pushed it, she realized it was a stupid thing to do, for now she would have to manoeuvre through the twisted hose and trailing cord when she ran down the stairs. But it turned out all right because the cord caught around the old man's feet as he raised his foot, and he fell. Even in her haste to escape, she tried not to let her feet touch any part of his prone body, for it would never do to kick one's father in-law. One was supposed to touch the dust of his feet and ask for his blessing. He reached out to catch her by her ankles and she almost tripped.

"What a vindictive old man," she shouted. "I just want to take what is mine and get out of this hell-hole," she said, shocking her mother-in-law. Menka, stupid woman, blocked her way to the front door. It would feel so good to give her a whack with the bat, she thought, but resisted. She went into the kitchen, and struck the floor instead. It felt so good, she whacked the door as well after she had opened the back door. Bhaiyan's second car was in the car porch and she was sorely tempted to whack her plastic bat and hear the sweet tinkle of glass. But Kanhaiya would not like that, she thought as she looked at the treasure in the crook of her arm. She ran out, cradling her Krishna, and slowed down to a walk as she entered the back lane. She knew the old man would come chasing, but she also knew he would take some time to change into street clothes. She turned left, then right, then left again, walking to a far bus stop, so as to throw him off if and when he came out of the house. She stepped into a gas station convenience store near the bus stop, and smiled at the cashier. "Good day to you," she said. "Could I use the restroom, please." He waved her in the right direction. Once in the washroom, where she had thought to leave the incriminating bat, she realized she had developed an attachment to it. She ran it under the faucet and wiped it off with toilet paper. She then came out, bought a chocolate bar and waited for the bus.

The first bus to come was headed towards Polo Park, but that was okay too.She crossed the street just in time, and got on. She made her way to the back and sat next to a teenager, even though there were many empty seats in the front.

"Nice day," she said. "I wonder if you could help me."

He grunted.

"Like, I am new to this country," she said.

He turned to give her a quick look and grunted.

She continued seriously, "and I really would like to learn some strong street language."

He cleared his throat. "Hmm," he said sarcastically,"to go with the bat, hn?"

"No, the real thing, not plastic like this bat."

He grunted.

"Like, 'beat the shit out of you', you know, some real stuff, "she said.

"Kick butt," he said.

"Kick butt," she repeated.

"Shoot some crap," he said.

"Shoot some crap," she repeated.

"Asshole."

"Asshole."

None of them sounded as good as her own contribution, 'beat the shit out of you'. But it didn't matter. There was time enough to learn. She took out the chocolate bar and offered it to him. "With thanks," she said.

"Hard to resist a KitKat," he said and took it.

"Know what?" he said. "You gotta be born to street language. Don't sound the same coming from you."

"Maybe you're right," she said. "Guess I'll just have to be my prim and proper Paki self."

"Heh," he said, grinning, "you're okay. My stop's coming up."

She turned her legs sideways and let him slide out. "Thanks for everything," she said.

"You're okay," he said. "Take care. I'd get rid of the bat, though."

She sat back, cradling Kanhaiya in her arms and holding the bat between her knees. She went all the way to the Polo Park terminus, then got out to read the route-maps on the walls of the bus shelter to see what bus she could take to go where. The choice seemed limitless. She went back to the driver of the bus she'd been on and said, "Excuse me, could you help me figure out how to get to Assiniboine Park?"

He told her.

"You've been very helpful," she said. "Have a wonderful day."

"Have a good life," he said.

A Selection of Our Titles in Print

A Lad from Brantford (David Adams Richards) essays	0-921411-25-1	11.95
All the Other Phil Thompsons Are Dead (Phil Thompson) poetry	1-896647-05-7	12.95
Avoidance Tactics (Sky Gilbert) drama	1-896647-50-2	15.88
CHSR Poetry Slam (Andrew Titus, ed.) poetry	1-896647-06-5	10.95
Combustible Light (Matt Santateresa) poetry	0-921411-97-9	12.95
Cover Makes a Set (Joe Blades) poetry	0-919957-60-9	8.95
Crossroads Cant (Mary Elizabeth Grace, Mark Seabrook, Shafiq, Ann Shin. Joe Blades, ed.) poetry	0-921411-48-0	13.95
Dark Seasons (Georg Trakl; Robin Skelton, trans.) poetry	0-921411-22-7	10.95
Elemental Mind (K.V. Skene) poetry	1-896647-16-2	10.95
for a cappuccino on Bloor (kath macLean) poetry	0-921411-74-X	13.95
Gift of Screws (Robin Hannah) poetry	0-921411-56-1	12.95
Heaven of Small Moments (Allan Cooper) poetry	0-921411-79-0	12.95
Herbarium of Souls (Vladimir Tasic) short fiction	0-921411-72-3	14.95
I Hope It Don't Rain Tonight (Phillip Igloliorti) poetry	0-921411-57-X	11.95
JC & Me (Ted Mouradian) religion	1-896647-35-9	15.99
Jive Talk: George Fetherling in Interviews and Documents George Fetherling (Joe Blades, ed.)	1-896647-54-5	13.95
Like Minds (Shannon Friesen) short fiction	0-921411-81-2	14.95
Manitoba highway map (rob mclennan) poetry	0-921411-8(-8	13.95
Memories of Sandy Point, St. George's Bay, Newfoundland (Phyllis Pieroway) memoir, history	0-921411-33-2	14.95
New Power (Christine Lowther) poetry	0-921411-94-4	11.95
Notes on drowning (rob mclennan) poetry	0-921411-75-8	13.95
Open 24 Hours (Anne Burke, D.C. Reid, Brenda Niskala Joe Blades, rob mclennan) poetry	0-921411-64-2	13.95
Railway Station (karl wendt) poetry	0-921411-82-0	11.95
Reader be Thou Also Ready (Robert James) novel	1-896647-26-X	18.69
Rum River (Raymond Fraser) short fiction	0-921411-61-8	16.95
Seeing the World with One Eye (Edward Gates) poetry	0-921411-69-3	12.95
Shadowy:Technicians: New Ottawa Poets (robmclennan, ed.) poetry	0-921411-71-5	16.95
Song of the Vulgar Starling (Eric Miller) poetry	0-921411-93-6	14.95
Speaking Through Jagged Rock (Connie Fife) poetry	0-921411-99-5	12.95
Starting from Promise (Lorne Dufour) poetry	1-896647-52-9	13.95
Tales for an Urban Sky (Alice Major) poetry	1-896647-11-1	13.95
The Longest Winter (Julie Doiron, Ian Roy) photos, fiction	0-921411-95-2	18.69
The Sweet Smell of Mother's Milk-Wet Bodice (Uma Parameswaran) novella	1-896647-72-3	13.95
Túnel de proa verde / Tunnel of the Green Prow (Nela Rio; Hugh Hazelton, translator) poetry	0-921411-80-4	13.95
Wharves and Breakwaters of Yarmouth County, Nova Scotia (Sarah Petite) art, travel	1-896647-13-8	17.95
What Morning Illuminates (Suzanne Hancock) poetry	1-896647-18-9	4.95
What Was Always Hers (Uma Parameswaran) fiction	1-896647-12-X	17.95

www.brokenjaw.com hosts our current catalogue, submissions guidelines, maunscript award competitions, booktrade sales representation and distribution information. Broken Jaw Press eBook of selected titles are available from http://www.PublishingOnline.Com. Directly from us, all individual orders must be prepaid. All Canadian orders must add 7% GST/HST (Canada Customs and Revenue Agency Number: 12489 7943 RT0001). **BROKEN JAW PRESS, Box 596 Stn A, Fredericton NB E3B 5A6, Canada**